THE OASIS

Mary McCarthy

THE OASIS

RANDOM HOUSE

NEW YORK

FIRST PRINTING

To Bowden

THE OASIS

> In fact, it must be confessed that, both in
> this world and the next, the wicked are al-
> ways a source of considerable embarrassment.
>
> From the passage on Mme de Warens'
> religious views in Rousseau's *Confessions*.

OBEDIENT to the social law that makes the
moot guest the early bird at a tea party, Mr.
and Mrs. Joseph Lockman were the first to
arrive in Utopia. The past cannot be discarded
in a single gesture, and Joe, in real life a diabetic business man from Belmont, Massachu-
setts, had spent thirty years beating his competitors to the jump. Joe's intentions toward
Utopia were already formidable: honoring its
principles of equality and fraternity, he was
nevertheless determined to get more out of it
than anybody else. This determination was
purely spiritual. Translated from his factory
and his garden to this heavenly mountain-top,

he intended to paint more, think more, and feel more than his co-colonists. He meant no evil by this; he called it leadership. He expected to be a spur and an incentive, as he had been to the brothers and the brothers-in-law in Lockman Leathergoods below. He would not have been in earnest about the higher life if he had failed to think of it in terms of the speed-up.

Habits die hard, particularly with the successful, and where the other colonists, defeated, for the most part, in their earthly endeavors by drink, pride, greed, caution, or laziness, looked upon Utopia as a concerted New Year's resolution, an insurrection of slaves against the inner masters, as well as a secession from society, Joe saw it simply as an extension of opportunity. He had always been a good man, and the only sin he had ever committed—the brother whom he had pronounced dead the day the shortage in the firm's accounts was discovered—he considered a righteous act. His one regret in real life, aside from family cares, was that he had not found sufficient time to give to his painting, a hobby he had taken up in middle age for purposes of relaxation, only to find in art (he had gone straight to the moderns) something bigger and better than business, a gigantic step-up transformer for the communication of personal electricity which excited his salesman's vision with promises of a vast "development." He looked forward with the greatest interest to the conversation of writers and painters, and it did not occur to him that he was participating in an anarchistic experiment. He knew himself to be a good mixer, as well as a good neighbor, and the communal program of the colony filled him, therefore, with no alarms—"What's mine is yours," he was fond of saying to acquaintances, and though he voted the Republican ticket, he had long been of the opinion that there was too much selfishness in the world. His exodus from Belmont, therefore, had an orderly and calmly transitional character. He had the AAA map out the route for him as usual, outlining the best highways in a serene wide ribbon of turquoise that ended abruptly, however, at the junction down in the valley, where the dirt road to Utopia trailed off from the numbered highway, anonymous and unmarked.

It was in the AAA office that Joe had experienced his first qualm. Before the blonde secretary, he felt really humiliated to think that Utopia did not figure on his Socony Automobile Guide. Etymology being one of his hobbies, he had already done the derivation of Utopia from *ou*, not, *topos*, a place ("Notaplace, get it?" he had said to his wife, Eva), yet the stare of the secretary unmanned him. He could not resist the impulse to put Utopia on the map. Seizing a pencil from the girl's desk, he had quickly drawn in a mountain where no surveyor had ever found one. "Look," he said. "Next year Socony will have it, right between Shaker Village and the birthplace of Stephen A. Douglas."

Afterwards, he was ashamed of what he had done. "Joe," he said to himself, in the hillbilly dialect he had adopted for interior disputation, "you hadn't ought to act thataway. What you care what folks think? We-uns up in the mountains don't give a damn about they-uns down in the valley." Self-parody was Joe's misfortune; he was a buffoon even with his soul. A sad Jewish comedian, grey-haired, grey-eyed, grey-skinned, sick, intelligent, unsure, he lacked audience-sense to an almost fatal degree. He used a dozen masks, accents, patters, soft-shoe steps, to parry an invisible laughter whose source he could not locate; in the confusion of these disguises, he had lost himself. The go-getting business man, the official greeter, the barber-shop harmonist, the Scout leader, the comic Englishman, Ikey the Jew, all these stereotypes were Joe's repertory, but they were also Joe. He had made himself grotesque for fear of becoming ridiculous, and though somewhere within him there was a voice crying in the wilderness, it spoke in a babel of tongues, in the base dialect of the Philistines. He was a prophet without honor to himself.

"He is the antithesis of everything we stand for," shouted Macdougal Macdermott, the editor of a libertarian magazine, the night Joe's name was proposed to the Utopian council. "My God, aren't we going to have any standards? I don't hold his business against him; he may be a decent employer; but, my God, the man is uncivilized. Don't you believe in *anything*? This fellow is a Yahoo." Ordinarily a generous-minded man, ready to oppose sectarianism whenever he observed it in others, Macdougal

Macdermott felt the proposed admission of Joe Lockman as a personal affront. Of all the enrolled Utopians, he was closest to Joe by temperament. Tall, red-bearded, gregarious, susceptible to a liver complaint, puritanical, disputatious, hard-working, monogamous, a good father and a good friend, he had suffered all his life from a vague sense that he was somehow crass, that he did not belong by natural endowment to that world of the spirit which his intellect told him was the highest habitation of man. That he could not *see* this world was a source of perpetual grievance to him; he knew that it existed through perceiving its effect on others, as a man in a snug house infers that the wind is blowing from the agitation of the leaves on the trees. Had he not seen a poem, he would have scoffed at the idea of poetry, and had the idea of poetry not been presented to him, he would have scoffed at a poem. Nevertheless, ten years before, he had made the leap into faith and sacrificed $20,000 a year and a secure career as a paid journalist for the intangible values that eluded his empirical grasp. He had moved down town into Bohemia, painted his walls indigo, dropped the use of capital letters and the practice of wearing a vest, and, having thus impressed his Sancho Panza into the service of quixotic causes, he now felt it to be the keenest ingratitude that he should be asked to admit into the fellowship a man who had done *nothing*. A whole habit of thrift in him cried out against the proposed largesse. Where was the justice in the world, if the savings of a lifetime were to be wiped out in a sudden inflation of the currency? Like the Prodigal Son's brother, he rebelled against this capriciousness of favor; his logical character cried out against the illogic of grace.

In the heat of the discussion that followed, two tendencies crystallized, the strict and the latitudinarian, and the strict would have won the day had not Mac himself, in one of those reversals of feeling characteristic of amateur parliaments, suddenly shifted ground. The ease with which his arguments were prevailing awoke him to question their validity; the novelty of winning a point put his dormant conscience on guard. He had been carried to the center of opinion more rapidly than he had

9

anticipated, and the very smoothness of the voyage made him distrust the current of passion that had swept him there. The elation of his supporters disgusted him and invoked a sympathy for Joe which persuasion could not have induced in him. "The man is human," he yelled, all at once, disregarding his previous contentions, just as though someone else had uttered them. "My God," he exclaimed, wheeling on his chief constituent, "what is this word, philistine? You talk as if he were an ape." "Mac," his supporter protested, "you're being inconsistent." "What if I am?" he shouted, waving his arms in the air. "You know what Emerson said. All right," he conceded, "I was wrong. The man has a right to exist." "And what," said Mrs. Macdermott, entering the argument unexpectedly, now that she found herself in agreement with her husband, and speaking in a quiet voice, "is Utopia but the right to a human existence?"

The others fell silent, mortified, recalled to their principles or to the principles, at any rate, of the colony, to which, however dubiously, with whatever reservations or secret hostilities,

they were lending a gingerly credence. A few
of the men grumbled, not because they disagreed with Mrs. Macdermott, but because they
grudged Mac Macdermott the luxury of being
both right and wrong in the same argument—
one opinion apiece was enough in a democracy.
And the placidity of Mrs. Macdermott's tone,
sounding into their discord, fretted them as
usual; Mrs. Macdermott, unlike the other colonists, had been born into New York society,
and though a gentle disposition and an identification with the unfortunate had given her
pretty, slight form and fragile pastel features
that downtrodden and even necessitous appearance so common among charitable women, she
still expressed herself in the secure manner of
one who has enjoyed advantages; the silver
spoon tinkled in her mouth whenever she spoke
against privilege. Retiring and diffident as she
was, she nevertheless appeared to feel herself as
a modest pivot at the very center of judgment,
and the long pale baby on her lap tonight, as
always, seemed to point the finger of reproach
at the less "responsible" members of the party—
the Macdermott children, naturally, had not

been made slaves of a schedule and enjoyed all the democratic freedoms, including the freedom of assembly.

"Eleanor's right!" Mac shouted, slapping his knee in delighted admiration. He applauded his wife thunderously, as if she were a team of acrobats, whenever she performed what to him was the extraordinary feat of arriving at a balanced opinion. His co-Utopians smiled. At bottom, they were grateful to Eleanor Macdermott for saving them from an act of ostracism which would indeed have been an ugly beginning for a community devoted to brotherhood. The incident, in fact, had frightened them a little. They had caught a glimpse of themselves in a mirror, a mirror placed at a turning-point where they had expected to see daylight and freedom, and though each of them, individually, was far from believing himself perfect, all had counted ·on the virtues of others to rescue them from themselves. They now felt somewhat dashed to find that they behaved (or had nearly behaved) worse together than any of them might have done singly, and, reluctantly dismissing from their minds the vision of Utopia as a kind of

12

collective security, they resolved that *from now on* (a phrase, alas, not new to any of them) they would set a guard on themselves and distrust their spontaneous feelings. There was no further debate about Joe Lockman, who was elected by acclamation—a good omen, everyone thought, for the success of the venture, for somehow, during the past half hour, Joe had become a symbol; the colony had found in this stray bird of the cormorant capitalist species, attaching itself so incongruously to their fortunes, its indispensable albatross.

Was it to follow then that *anyone* could be admitted to Utopia—a thief, a blackmailer, a murderer? Why not, declared the purists, arguing for the life of risk and the precedent of the bishop's candlesticks. Impossible, said the realists: the physical survival of the colony was more important than a mere demonstration of principle—a strong and self-confident Utopia could perhaps afford a murderer, but a Utopia not yet consolidated must defer this luxury until a later date. Fortunately, perhaps, the point remained academic. No murderers or thieves applied, only ordinary people of ordinary B plus morality, people whose crimes that is, had been confined to an intimate circle, and who had never injured anybody but a close friend, a relation, a wife, a husband, themselves. There were no saints in Utopia, and none who believed themselves saintly. The only saint with whom the colonists were personally acquainted had disappeared in a darkened city of Europe and was believed by the American consul to be, very probably, dead.

To members of the purist faction, the absence of this man was terrible, for it was from him, an Italian anarchist in possession of his first papers, a veteran of the Spanish war and of Vichy's prisons, a lover of Plato and Tolstoy, a short pink-and-black man with a monk's tonsure of baldness and a monk's barrel chest, that they had learned certain notions of justice, freedom, and sociability which now, long after he had left them, they were endeavoring to illustrate in action. The realistic party, on the other hand, while sympathizing vividly with his American wife (far more indeed than the purists, who thought principally of the loss to themselves) and urging attention to the case upon various acquaintances in the State Department, regarded the absence of the Founder as, on the whole, a blessing. They feared, above everything else, that Utopia, like Oneida, Brook Farm, and the phalansteries, would make itself a laughing-stock by the advocacy of extreme ideas. To them Utopia was justified on sheerly practical grounds, as a retreat from atomic warfare, a summer-vacation colony, a novelty in personal relations; and though in their hearts they too hoped for some millennial outcome of the experiment, for the reign of justice and happiness, they shrank from a definition of the colony which committed them to any positive belief. Conspicuous goodness, like the Founder's, filled them with uneasy embarrassment; they looked upon it as a form of simple-mindedness on a par with vegetarianism, and would have refused admission to Heaven on the ground that it was full of greenhorns and cranks.

That the purists had different ideas about Utopia, the realists were well aware, and well aware too that there existed in the other faction certain plans for their moral transformation in which they had not been included. That the other side was banking on the isolation of the mountain-top, the soft influences of Nature, the gentle admonitions of example, to bring out the best in them, they had seen from the beginning. But they had no intention of being changed or improved, and they smiled among themselves at this childish conspiracy, which seemed to them the final proof of their opponents' naïveté. The prospect of remaining unregenerate and defeating the purists' hopes excited in them a mood of zestful anticipation; it gave salt to the whole project, which otherwise they would have found insipid.

The dark features of Will Taub, leader of the realist party, had contorted into an expression of malicious triumph when he heard that a lady purist had lightly pronounced him "salvageable." "Idiots!" he thunderously proclaimed, pounding his fist on his coffee-table, upsetting a highball over the manuscript of a rather proprietary article on Tocqueville which he was preparing for the press. Up to this moment, he had been uncertain as to whether or not to blacklist Utopia, and his visitor, in fact, had relied on the bit of gossip to goad him into

16

a decision, for, like many other spiteful people who infested Bohemian circles during that era, the busybody now seated on Taub's sofa was actively campaigning against the formation of a colony which threatened no interest of his and was wholly pacific and benevolent, so that long before Utopia had crystallized, an anti-Utopian movement of the most definite character existed, and men and women were calling on their friends, trying to dissuade them from the project, against which their only conceivable grudge was the fear of not being invited, and giving more time and energy to this cause than they had ever been able to summon up for the fight say, against fascism or Stalinism. In the case of Will Taub, however, the visitor had made an error. He was not sufficiently versed in his host's ingenious psychology to guess that the slug which he had just inserted in the mechanism would hit the jackpot, but in a manner quite unexpected. *"Salvage,"* Taub softly exclaimed. "I'd like to see that," and he gave the peculiar short harsh laugh that was indicative of his polemical humor. "We'll go," he abruptly announced, tapping his wife familiarly on the shoulder, as if to apprise her that a show was about to begin into which he had privately written a sardonic star part for himself. His wife, inured to surprises, merely raised her penciled eyebrows. Taub's imagination continued to work. "What *fools* they'll make of themselves. It will be *marvelous*," he cried, nudging his visitor this time, and rolling slightly on the sofa. The tip of his tongue fastened itself against his lower teeth, and the center broadened and protruded in a truly malignant fashion as he emitted another grating laugh, vainglorious and taunting. "A-a-ah," he exclaimed, and the visitor, half-forgotten, felt embarrassed and even slightly frightened by the directness of this hostility. "It was quite strange," he later declared. "He positively stuck his tongue out. Do you think I was wrong to tell him? I feel quite alarmed for the Utopians."

Yet Will Taub in reality was not wholly displeased by the remark which had been repeated to him. Something shy and childlike in his nature felt obscurely flattered by the judgment. He and his whole party, to tell the truth, would have been glad to be redeemed or "salvaged," if this could only be accomplished privately, and without the loss of that ideological supremacy which had become essential to their existence. As inheritors of "scientific" socialism, they based themselves on Marx and Engels, and though they had discarded the dialectic and the labor theory of value and repudiated with violence whatever historical process was going on behind the iron curtain, their whole sense of intellectual assurance rested on the fixed belief in the potency of history to settle questions of value. The failure of socialism in their time, the ascendancy of the new slave state were for them, therefore, an excruciating personal humiliation. To identify their survival with the arms of Western capitalism had been a natural step, but one which they took uneasily and with a certain semantic embarrassment—they showed far less constraint in characterizing the opponents of this policy as childish, unrealistic, unhistorical, etc., than in formulating a rhetoric of democratic ideals.

They had accepted as their historic mission the awakening of the left to the dangers of Red totalitarianism, and this task, with the aid of actual developments, they had accomplished with credit, but history itself (surely their real enemy) had superseded them, taking matters into its own hands, while the ungrateful left had failed to reward them with the unquestioning trust and obedience which they felt to be the logical sequel, and kept demanding, in articles, book reviews and private conversation, that they produce new ideas or else yield place to their juniors. As they patiently searched out the pages of Marx and Engels for precedents for a policy of "critical support" to governments, others, more reckless than they, hurried on ahead of them to rediscover the blessings of capitalism; still others remained obstinately true to the axioms of the socialist textbook—protection for minorities, opposition to wars and governments—and a third group, most recusant, tried to reject the whole of materialist doctrine and either to embrace religion or to assert, in small groups outside the main current, man's power to dwell in relative harmony and justice. In most of these deviations, there was a common factor, an assumption of human freedom, which the realistic party felt it its duty to combat.

In practice, of course, Taub and his friends conceded to anyone (this automatically excluded fascists and communists) the liberty of behaving as ineffectually as he wished. But the right of a human being to *think* that he could resist history, environment, class structure, psychic conditioning was something they denied him with all the ferocity of their own pent-up natures and disappointed hopes. The idea that there was a loophole by which others were escaping while they themselves played trustees to the law of cause and effect drove them to a fury that they could hardly rationalize. Thus they were at once the victims and the masters of a doctrine of inevitability. The dictators of a diminishing circle of literary and political thinkers, they maintained the habit of authority by a subservience to events, demonstrating irrefutably that an occurrence that had already happened could not have happened otherwise and translating this security into predictions of the future. They had been for some time more or less inactive politically, and their materialism had hardened into a railing cynicism, yet they still retained from their Leninist days, along with the conception of history as arbiter, a notion of themselves as a revolutionary *élite* whose correctness in political theory allowed them the widest latitude in personal practice. The misdeeds which they obstinately defended against the attacks of "morality" were, as a matter of fact, of the most trivial and commonplace character, quite lacking in social *élan*, yet the faction was committed to these failings as if to a higher principle. They could not repent them, though repentance might have afforded relief, and they could not embark openly upon a new course of conduct, lest their whole past, in this light, appear unjustified. They were thus in a desperate situation, for their position, while unassailable from without, offered no egress either. They had grown to dislike criticism so heartily that even self-criticism struck them as a form of *lèse-majesté*; with crushing arguments, they refused the inner voice before it had finished speaking. This did not prevent them from feeling dissatisfied and unhappy, maligned and misunderstood; it only increased their sense of being surrounded by hostile forces. Time and age also, they felt, were conspiring to make them ridiculous; in business, once they had entrenched themselves in sinecures with an air of majestic astuteness, they soon found themselves discomfited precisely by their "executive" leisure and feared, above everything else, the eyes of their hard-working subordinates which seemed to be calculating their deficit on some impersonal adding machine.

The necessity of going to an office, indeed, had become a source of genuine grievance with them. They felt positively imposed upon by the *fact* of an exploited class through whose room they were obliged to pass going and coming from lunch, arriving late on Mondays and leaving for the week-end on Thursdays. They were short and harsh with the typists, rude to the telephone girls; they slipped in and out without saying good day, found querulous fault with their secretaries, and beefed confidentially to them about the onerousness of the work. The more unpopular they knew themselves, the more they felt called upon to exercise—as a declaration of freedom—those very prerogatives which were the cause of resentment. All of this was quite at variance with their private characters, which were expansive and easy-going, if somewhat inclined to sloth. As realists, however, they were in no position to assert that the office self they presented, made up as it was simply of actions, was false to the inner picture. These tribulations had decidedly soured their tempers, and the compromises they had made in adjusting themselves to the "realities" of capitalism appeared to them sometimes in the light of a supreme sacrifice, a sacrifice quite unappreciated by Macdermott and his circle of irresponsible moralists, toward whom despite nominal friendship they felt a slow and vengeful anger like the rancor of the veteran toward the artful draft dodger.

Thus their wish to see Utopia fail was sincere and even righteous; they looked forward to its debacle with a true Old Testament fervor and were prepared to go down themselves, like Samson with the temple of the Philistines, in vindication of the reality principle which remained the sole justification of their otherwise miscalculated lives. At the same time, they wished to do nothing to provoke the disaster which they fore-

24

saw; a sense of fair play, a feeling for scientific method which made them look on Utopia as an experiment which must be conducted under rigidly controlled conditions in order that the outcome they predicted should appear as the inevitable result, resolved them to give the colony the benefit of the doubt, to behave toward it peaceably and co-operatively, and not get the name of obstructionists. The very caution of this reasoning edged the door ajar to salvation, but only the purists discerned this and rejoiced at their opponents' error. The point eluded Will Taub, who had persuaded himself that he was entering Utopia in a spirit of adamant scepticism, and had stipulated nothing more than to be *on his good behavior* at the preliminary council meetings. That this formula represented for him at that moment the zenith of ethical strivings, he was not aware, but sometimes, during a council meeting, shooting a suspicious glance at the demure and earnest face of one of his allies, Taub could not be sure that *he* was not the dupe and that his whole faction had not bamboozled him and gone over to the purist side. And even in himself he discovered a certain mood of armistice which confirmed his alarms and which at the same time was not displeasing to him—a sense of generosity and of the protocol of forbearance. He participated in the forms of equity with increasing confidence, and though of course he did not take any of it *seriously*, his heavy and rather lowering nature performed the unaccustomed libertarian movements with a feeling of real sprightliness and wondering self-admiration, as if he had been learning to dance. He did not encourage his wife to attend these council-meetings and, coming home in the evenings, spoke of what had passed with a brief snort of disparagement; from this she was able to perceive that his emotions had become involved.

On the day set for the great migration, therefore, the Utopian prospect looked brighter than an outsider might have supposed. The party of mechanized pilgrims guiding their family cars up the rutted road to Utopia was by no means entirely composed of the two factions, but included an assortment of persons of diffuse and uncommitted good will, two editors of a national news weekly, a Latinist teacher of boys who practised a Benedictine Catholicism, an unemployed veteran of the Second World War, a girl student, a Protestant clergyman, a trade union publicist, several New York high-school teachers, an alcoholic woman illustrator, an unmarried private secretary who would organize games for the children, a middle-aged poet who had once been a Southern agrarian, an actor and a radio script-writer whom no one could remember voting for. All these, together with their husbands and wives, made up the Utopian center, voting sometimes with the realists and sometimes with the purists, inclining, naturally enough, a little to the purist side (otherwise they would hardly have been there) but siding with the realists on several important issues, the exclusion, for instance, of communists from the membership, an issue which had temporarily created a new alignment of forces, the Latinist, the radio writer, the clergyman, and the ex-agrarian backing up the realists, to everyone's surprise, while the two magazine editors, who had their own brand of realism, the horse-sense, let's-look-at-the-facts-boys, indigenous American type, had spoken out very strongly on the purist side.

"Cross your bridges when you come to them," handsome editor Haines had advised. "Don't commit yourself unless you have to. Let's see how we feel when a Commie wants in." This argument and, above all, Jim Haines's seasoned and sagacious manner of unfolding it convinced the colony of the practical wisdom of following his prescription. The purists believed they had won, and the middle-of-the-roaders were content that the colony should keep its principles at least until the moment when it became necessary to apply them, a moment that seemed remote, since any communists who were not in the hands of the authorities were, according to common knowledge, infiltrating the subterranean armament factories, drilling subversively in the training-camps, or enrolled in America Last, an anti-war organization so reactionary that it had not yet been certified as disloyal.

Utopia was too small a movement—it comprised only fifty persons—to serve the communist interest by obstructing the national war drive. It had hopes of extending its influence by

28

inspiring other persons to form oases of their own in the contemporary desert, but the flag of secession it raised was no Fort Sumter. It had been investigated by the Attorney General as a possible communist front group (one of its enemies having denounced it as "objectively" giving aid to communism), but the case against it had been dropped, since the worst that could be said against it was that most of its membership had been guilty of "premature" anti-Stalinism. Pacifism had not yet been made a crime, providing that the pacifist was above the age to bear arms or suffered from some physical disability. The Administration was doing its best to preserve some vestiges of civil liberties (it was badly in need of war aims), and it could point to its toleration of Utopia with patriotic complacency. Moreover, the Home Defense Authority had been urging decentralization as an anti-air raid measure; it was not against the law for a group of people to move together to the country; the Utopians could not even be said to be violating a zoning ordinance. The men and women of the colony had registered with their draft boards as agricultural workers;

the children were too young to qualify for the service; there was not a doctor or a scientist among the colonists; all of them, in fact, were quite "unnecessary" people, even Will Taub, who had offered himself to the State Department as an expert on communist strategy, only to endure the scrutiny of a pair of plainclothes detectives, to have his wires tapped and his tax-returns opened to question, and to be told in the end that his arsenal of ideas was rusty, since he had lost contact with the Party at the time of the Spanish Civil War.

Up to the last minute, the colonists found it impossible to believe that society was going to let them depart with so little molestation, as if to say, "Go in peace." The realists suspected a trap, and the more intransigent members asked themselves what Monteverdi, the Founder, would have said if he could have seen that cavalcade of cars, well stocked with whisky, cans, and contraceptives, winding up the mountain of Nowhere with their papers in perfect order—doubtless, he would have smiled but they could hardly smile for him, and the evocation of his fate cast, for those who had loved him, a shadow on the

Utopian hillside, comparable to the shadow of Calvary upon the militant Church. Reviewing their actions, however, in the light of the ideas of the Founder, they could find no real cause for self-reproach. Throughout, in every decision, they had respected the idea of *limit*, which seemed to them in retrospect the very definition of his thought. Agreeing, in principle, that the machine was to be distrusted, they had nevertheless voted to use in their experiment the bicycle, the carpet-sweeper, and the sewing-machine, any machine, in fact, to which a man contributed his own proportionate share of exertion and which tired him like the plough or the hoe. The bath, the flush toilet, all forms of plumbing they tolerated, but they opposed, at least for the time being, the installation of an electric power-plant, proposing to cook by wood and read in the evenings by oil, and to avail themselves of an old ice-house they had found on the property they were buying to solve the very stubborn problem of refrigeration. To their traveling by automobile, Monteverdi could have raised no objection (the trip had to be made somehow), and accused of inconsistency by their enemies, they could argue that they looked upon the family car as Lenin in 1917 looked upon the sealed car offered him by the German State to reach insurrectionary Petersburg—as a vehicle to the future appropriated from the past, the negation of a negation.

Everything could be explained—the whisky, the contraceptives, the collection of summer fashions being imported by a lady purist—for it was a by-law of this unique Utopia that every member be allowed to bring whatever was necessary to his happiness: he defined himself freely by his choices and could not allege social conformity as an excuse for his personal passions. And out of those loaded automobiles began to come a variety of definitions of happiness: happiness as ornament, happiness as utility, happiness as oblivion, happiness as squalor, happiness in a small suitcase, happiness in giving (Joe Lockman's Cadillac carried presents for every family), in a French casserole or a sterilizer, a kiddie-coop or a gold evening dress, Spanish shawls, books, pictures, batik hangings, porch furniture, blue jeans, garden tools, carpentry sets, a single tennis racket forever to go unpartnered, a Greek dictionary, Homer and Plato, Elizabethan songs; happiness even arrived, somewhat later, in a moving van carrying two grand pianos and a Chinese Chippendale sideboard.

To Susan Hapgood, a young novelist, walking on the central lawn with Will Taub, her literary adviser, the scene of the unpacking had all the charms of fiction. Loving only books and conversation, she had already disposed of her small effects in the quarter-cottage allotted to her, and was taking her second pleasure in the expansive company of Taub, who strolled up and down, hands behind his back, surveying the effects of his colleagues with undisguised wonder. A transparent air of proprietorship emanated from his whole person; to his fellow-colonists he suggested a summer hotel manager, with his large, city feet clad in new white shoes which creaked even on the grass and betrayed his every movement, a hotel manager, however, in whom curiosity had mastered discretion and who, like an ingenuous bell-boy, could not refrain from comment on the objects, so foreign to his experience, so peculiar in shape and mysterious in utility, on which other persons had obviously placed value. Susan, running along beside him, was experiencing emotions of a different order. Her blue eyes widened and her small mouth emitted sharp cries of literary admiration as each article, when unpacked, added an inspired touch to the characterization of its owner, as though all these domestic details had been endowed with the faculty of surprising convincingly by an Author supremely clever. Who would have thought that the Latinist possessed a pair of boxing gloves? Or that Macdermott was inseparable from a snoreball? (Susan was a generous critic.)

"Why, it's just like going to a fire," she exclaimed in her plain, small-town voice, whose commonplace timbre delighted the ears of her Eastern friends and made them treat her with protective tenderness, like a fresh farm egg delivered to their kitchens. "You sit across the street and watch the family's belongings carried out to the lawn by the fire department," she added, perceiving Taub's doubtful expression. "That must be marvelous," he cried, as he rolled the possibilities of this appreciatively over the tongue of his fancy. Facts of any kind, oddities, lore, local history intoxicated the mind of this realist, whose own experience had been strangely narrow—a half-forgotten childhood in the Carpathian mountains, immigration, city streets, the Movement, Bohemian women, the anti-Movement, downtown bars, argument, discussion, subways, newsstands, the office. This was all he knew of the world; the rest was hearsay, upon which his materialist imagination was continually at play, building on straws of report vast structures of conjecture and speculation. He was a theorist *faute de mieux*, for what really interested him was information and the magical properties it contained for the armchair subjugation of experience. People's ideas bored him, once he had placed them in his atlas; he was a politician even with thought, keeping an eye on the various developments in literature and the arts in the manner of a chief of State who has some subordinate read aloud to him the editorials in the opposition newspapers and cuts him off impatiently, after a few sentences, when the tendency of the article is clear to him.

Susan, now, would have been glad to turn away; her conscience was already punishing her for the sin of inordinate curiosity; she felt she had seen too much. But Taub found himself utterly captivated by the spectacle of his fellow-colonists' worldly goods spread out on the grass for his inspection. He would have liked to finger them candidly, like some child with a naturalistic bent who sees no harm in the impulse which his elders are always correcting. "Come away," Susan kept repeating. "Let's go help Cynthia unpack." She began to tug at his arm, and Taub reluctantly yielded, as the others started glancing their way. Wariness returned to him; he buttoned his face hastily as if correcting a negligence in his dress. Concealment was second nature to him (though he had nothing to hide): he liked confidences, closed rooms, low voices; his eyelids were normally drooped and his gaze darted out between them, following events narrowly, like a watcher behind shutters. He felt annoyed now with Susan for the demonstrativeness of her manners, but this did not really darken the mood of almost sententious satisfaction he felt in the afternoon's doings. He had found out many things he had not known before; further possibilities still opened; there was much to be learned. A part of his antipathy toward the colony had sprung simply from the fear of boredom—Macdermott and a pack of schoolteachers and religious types, what had they got to say to him that he had not heard before? He could read it all in Macdermott's magazines, in a series called New Roads, without paying rent on a cottage and being put to work on the land. He had forgotten the perennial fascination exercised over him by behaviour. The tree of life, he said to himself, quoting Hegel, is greener than the tree of thought. (His eye caught the girl-student sitting cross-legged in front of her cottage and ingested her long legs; Susan watched them move bulgingly down the tract of his appreciation, like a snake's dinner, to join the Jacksons' English bicycles and the breasts of the minister's wife.)

It is not only, Taub reflected as they passed on and his mood grew more and more serene, that life is more fertile than the brain: we applaud Nature when she repeats herself, while we do not forgive this in a speaker. The capacity of personality to run true to form, of a plant to reproduce its characteristics, is a source of joy to the intelligence. If Macdermott tells me that violence is wrong, I wait for him to say something new, but if every carton in his second-hand car repeats the label, Economy Size, I am obviously delighted. Here Taub frowned and abandoned the line of thought, for the Scotch joke had reminded him of the fact that he was Jewish, a painful subject with him, the source of much unhappiness, unguessed at by his friends, who did not know that they wounded his pride every time they mentioned the word Jew, or described some instance of anti-Semitism, which cut him to the heart. A kind of helplessness came over him when he became conscious of his Jewishness, a thing about himself which he was powerless to alter and which seemed to reduce him therefore to a curious dependency on the given. He was not a defiant Jew or even a rebellious one. At such moments, he felt himself to be a mere mass of protoplasmic jelly, deposited by the genes of his parents, which could only quiver feebly in response to a stimulus that society sent through him like an electric current. He began suddenly, as he always did on these occasions, to long for his wife, a Gentile woman who alone understood what he suffered on this score, and who had never, during all their years together, alluded to it unsolicited. For this tact he felt a gratitude toward her that was mingled with surprise and reverence. She held a unique place in his heart, though he consulted her convenience seldom, was brusque and out-of-sorts with her when she tried to think about social problems. A reserved girl who designed clothes, she spoke very little at parties, and many rivals had been encouraged to hope by her silence and apparent coldness. What they did not perceive was that Taub trusted her without reserve; he had put his Jewishness into her Gentile hands and she had never used it against him. This trust meant more to him, a political man, than all the allurements of her competitors. He could rely on her absolutely, in the manner of those antique sovereigns who kept at their right hand a Gaul, a Greek, or an Egyptian, some scion of the traditional enemy, a slave, often, or a hostage, whose allegiance they felt the more sure of because it transcended the bounds of custom and thereby partook of the improbable—generally, in their histories, the stranger has let pass an opportunity to kill the tyrant, and the tyrant has been stirred, in the very depths of his self-love, by the *gratuitousness* of this fealty. The romance of Cyrus and Xenophon, of Caesar and Diviciacus the Haeduan, of the Doge of Venice and Othello, were recapitulated in the Taub marriage, which naturally was childless. All Taub's paternal feelings (and he was at bottom a fatherly man) spent themselves on the *fact* of his foyer, which was sanctified for him, like a child. He marveled clumsily over table-settings and sofas, as a father does over the feats of a baby, and felt toward his furnishings even that doubt and apprehension experienced by the head of the household toward the nursery routines of the infant (did his wife really know what she was doing?—it had not been that way in his childhood).

Something of this watchful benevolence, now, he transferred to the whole colony. Standing alone on the peak (he had dropped Susan at her cottage several minutes before) listening to the evening sounds, the cries of the children being fed, the wood being chopped for the stoves, he laughed aloud to himself in sheer victorious contentment. His mind explored sensuously the realm of possibility that lay outstretched at his feet: across the valley, a herd was grazing on a knoll; smoke came from the chimney of a farmhouse; fences, the barking of a dog, a ploughed field cut neatly into sections gave a sense of the human scale, reduced by distance to miniature, like a toy agricultural set; while far off, through the cleft of the valley, ranges and ranges of mountains, bare, grand, and purple, topped one another just distinguishably and disappeared finally into the horizon, carrying the vision outward into apocalyptic space. All this Taub's eye appropriated; his soul enlarged to its measure, as he stood outlined against the sky, Balboa claiming for his orthodoxy the whole mode of the pacific—he felt like Utopia's discoverer and an impresario to Nature.

This Te Deum swelling in Taub's heart reverberated throughout the colony. The membership was tranquilly a-hum in the abandoned summer resort, a three-story hotel with cottages done in the Swiss chalet style which had failed many years before, during the First World War, been half renovated in the late thirties and left to stand as it was, when gas-rationing and the shortage of food condemned it for summer-vacationing and the seashore replaced the mountains as the American playground. Beds, chairs, lamps, washstands, screens, of the era of the resort's short popularity, remained in their places; flour and meal and sugarbins, iron and granite-ware pots, flame-toasters and waffle-irons stood ready to hand in the big kitchen; rusted irons in the laundry challenged the more adventurous women to clean them and heat them on the stove. It was as if the hotel and its furnishings had been arrested at the magical moment of the average birth-date of the colonists nearly forty years before, and arrested also, conveniently, at the stage of mechanization to which the colonists wished to return. A whole system of life stood waiting to be resumed, a point which had persuaded the realists to submit to the purists' ideology, particularly since the drafting of labor and the scarcity of materials, owing to the oncoming war, put large-scale modernization in any case out of the question. And the realists too, of both tendencies, were not insensitive to the charm of the fresh start, so aptly symbolized in the old hotel and its appliances, which took them back to the age of their innocence, to the dawn of memory, and the archaic figures of Father and Mother. Here, for the moment, it seemed to all of them that it was possible to begin over again from the beginning and correct the small error that was responsible for the vast confusion, like the single mistake made at any early stage in a mathematical calculation which accounts for a difference of billions in the final answer.

It was not, as their enemies alleged, that the colonists desired to turn the clock back once and for all; it pleased them, rather, to set it at the moment of their entrance onto the human scene, clean it, and start it going again. They might have set it earlier or later—the Catholic scholar, for example, would have preferred, at least in theory, to go back before Copernicus, and the long-legged girl student imagined that the first Roosevelt Administration had been the high point of human achievement. To some,

43

the errors to be rectified were largely of a personal nature: Ed Jackson, drinking from the spring, stepping deep into wild forget-me-nots, recovered a lost sensation, the pure, keen thirst of his boyhood, and knew that reform was still possible if water could give him such a kick. To others, it was not so much their own sins, but the burden of social error that seemed to drop from their shoulders—Versailles, Spain, Munich, Yalta, the failure of the socialist movement, all these massive objective factors with which they had had to contend in a struggle increasingly hopeless, the dead weight of decisions taken in the world capitals which had the power of changing their lives without being changed by them, decisions which rested not on the popular will but on the resignation of a public which, despite the ballot-box, looked upon wars and social catastrophes as the medieval peasant looked upon cholera and earthquake, as manifestations of fatality, afflictions from the Beyond. Here, at any rate, the premises of action were the colonists' own; here the mistakes of Kautsky, Lenin, Wilson, Chamberlain, Roosevelt, Attlee, Truman, Dewey, not to mention the crimes of Hitler, Stalin, Franco, Mussolini, were not, so to speak, dealt out to them as the cards they were forced to play with, or else get out of the game. They shuffled their own deck, and even the realists, who saw the doom of the venture in some practical joker they called "human nature," expected this joker to assert itself in the behavior of the colonists themselves and not somewhere outside them, in the inscrutable order of things.

The recovery, if only in token, of a world small and self-contained, had, that first night, an exhilarating effect, and the presence of very obvious difficulties of a practical sort only enlivened the membership to meet and answer the challenge. The committee in charge of housing had been prepared for a great many complaints; it received nothing but praise. To many of the members, the discovery that they could do without their comforts came as a delightful surprise, as though the material objects which had been subtracted from their bodies were added, by way of compensation, to their moral girth. For a majority, material life in the real world had been easy, relatively speaking, and mental life hard; the reversal of this relation gave birth to a sense of resourcefulness long missing from their spirits. The limits of their mental capacities they knew all too well. They had yet to find the limits of their physical powers, but the disclosure that he could trim a wick, say, was an almost overwhelming experience for a man who had felt sick with fear whenever the electric company wrote him that the power would be turned off if the bill were not paid by the fifteenth. *Independent action* became, for the first time that night, something more than a phrase; the most impetuous spirits went racing ahead in their talk to a moment when the colony would produce not only its own eggs, milk, butter, cheese, hams, vegetables and bacon, but furniture, shoes, and clothing. The idea that for certain things—oil, paper, medicines—they would always be beholden to society nearly brought tears to their eyes, as it collided sharply with their fancy, though they had faced it calmly enough back there in the city, where any improvement in their condition seemed almost too much to ask for. A *complete break* with the present was already being envisioned in some

46

quarters before the first egg had been laid, and one purist, going for milk, was arguing with another the propriety of their action, since according to the by-laws a herd should have been delivered on the day of their arrival—a firm line must be taken or they would soon be buying store-bread at the filling-station down below.

Joe Lockman was the only one in the group to be genuinely disturbed by the regression, as he thought of it, to an age of inconvenience. He was an old hand at roughing it—that was not the trouble. Just to show the stuff he was made of, he had spent the whole afternoon with his scythe, subduing the Utopian hillside, working at top speed and with no variation of pace, leaving havoc behind him and alarm in the minds of his colleagues, who did not understand the motive for such a wholesale act of destruction. The signs of industry in his fellows—a man mowing the lawn and another putting up a hammock; a husband driving in clothes-poles and a wife hanging curtains in her window—he had watched with favor, interrupting his work to come down and give a word of advice ("Just let me have that lawn-mower a minute, young man, and I'll show you how to do it"). Something, nevertheless, in the prevailing attitude did not smell right to him. It struck him that the colonists were virtually playing house. It made him quite uneasy to see those old lyre-backed wicker chairs dragged out so joyfully onto the lawn; he remembered them perfectly from his youth and regretted not having brought his foam-rubber glider from Belmont, brand-new last autumn and a thousand times more comfortable. All those oohs and ahs over the woodstoves and the waffle-irons sounded forced in his ears—could anyone honestly mean them? His wife hated cooking and would never adjust herself to using those clumsy old devices. Ever since the Second War, they had been doing without a regular maid; she seemed to prefer it that way, now that the children's rooms were empty, just the two of them alone in the house. She liked bakery cakes, ready mixes, redispreads, rolls from the delicatessen; she often had him stop at the S. S. Pierce cold meat counter or the Home Foods department at Schrafft's on Tremont Street to bring in something for supper. A nice little steak or some chops she did not mind doing, and Sundays, if she had to, if the parents were coming to dinner, she would put her roast in a self-basting pan, set the thermometer on the oven, and go upstairs to lie down. He knew Eva's habits very well, and he could see that she was not going to get along at all with these younger women ecstasizing over bread tins and butter churns.

Eva's objections, however, were not the paramount question. Guessing how things would be, he had left an order with S. S. Pierce to send them a weekly food package—canned fruit, hams, hard salamis, smoked salmon, sandwich mixes, and a bottle or two of sparkling burgundy to be slipped in by a friendly clerk. His wife's niceties and nerves, her hostilities and resistance to change he had jollied along for years; he almost loved them in her, identifying them with the womanly; he thought her more fastidious than himself and her aversion to the outdoors, he took for a mark of superiority, like her linen pumps and her nylons and her bad times of the month. That Eva would be out of her element here, he had accepted from the start; only the imminent war had made her consent to accompany him; and he was grateful enough for her presence to resign himself to her disapproval, though even now, despite thirty years of experience, he would not quite part with the hope (which he chided in himself as treasonable) that the caustic little queen of his household could become the comrade of his pleasures. But an allegiance even more profound than what he owed his wife's happiness was being shaken by the behavior of the Utopians. His loyalty to the modern was challenged.

The modern, with Joe, was a true passion and a cause, something more than a painter's convention or a designer's style. A great personal sincerity invested his feelings on this subject, for he was already a modern painter before he discovered the modern movement; the few lessons he had had in a business man's art club in Boston had taught him only what he now called "a sterile academicism"—he had had to work out his idiom alone in his own backyard. The coincidence between his own efforts and the paintings of the School of Paris, pointed out to him finally by his amazed children, convinced him of the authenticity of the revelation he had

had. Under the influence of a teacher who gave lessons in art by correspondence, he came quickly to believe that the modern was some sort of duty laid on every man who had heard its call, a system of knowledge and perception equivalent to revealed religion—and for all those born too early to receive its message, for Raphael and Shakespeare, he felt a kind of pity like that of the pious Christian for the deprived souls of the ancients, who died too soon to get the benefit of the Redemption. The routines of factory and family life, much as he respected them, had long impeded his progress in spontaneous self-expression, so that the summons to Utopia, when it came, had reached him like an awaited signal. When his son felt it necessary to warn him that the colonists held advanced opinions, Joe at once prepared himself for a rigorous testing of his convictions in the crucible of practice. He had flexed his will for cabins built like iceboxes, steel chairs or none, a long communal table in the shape of a streak of lightning, people reciting poems and wearing eccentric costumes, free love even, and the children running about naked.

Nothing could have been better calculated to disturb his preconceptions than the 1910 summer hotel into which he found himself moving his drawing board. Of all periods in American history, the age of Taft made the least appeal to his imagination; he remembered it too well for it to hold for him any charm or mystery. Progress, in fact, to his mind, was measured against that era. Electric light, radio, television, labor-saving devices for the housewife, the abolition of piece-work, the tractor, all the benefits to mankind that had been developed within his memory, seemed to him to have ameliorated beyond estimate the life of the average person; and though he believed that there had been some tendency to substitute mechanical pleasure for *living* (a favorite doctrine with him), to depend too uncreatively on the juke-box, the movies, and the automobile, he considered this merely a misapplication of inventions basically good. He knew that he himself could set off tomorrow with a bowie-knife and a compass and forge out a life for himself, should atomic raids oblige it, but he was too chivalrous to dream of this as a solution for the problems of mankind in general (what would become of poor Eva?), and the idea that the splitting of the atom was in any way evil in itself had never entered his mind. The derogation of technology that was going on all around him was something strange to his ears; it struck him as slightly blasphemous, and he hoped that his wife would not hear it. The notion, moreover, that the past thirty-five years, the whole of his adult life, had been mis-spent by society, a notion that seemed to be cur-rent on the lawn, in the kitchen, in the lounge, filled him with consternation. He felt disillu-sioned with the colonists and did not know what to think.

On the porch, waiting for Eva to call him to supper (irregular meals were bad for a diabetic condition), he experienced a sudden antagonism to Macdougal Macdermott, who sat laughing over a yellowed newspaper with a picture of a doughboy on the front page. Joe himself had fought in that war; indeed, his manhood had been seasoned in it—today, in his son's old fatigue uniform, rolled up in the legs, with his slightly belligerent stance, he looked the veteran still, though grey and almost visibly aging, as though time were galloping through him like a horse racing to the finish. *Amour propre* urged him to insist that the first war had been necessary (he was not so sure about the second, in which his son had been wounded—Hitler, he thought now, should have been stopped in the Rhineland), but his positiveness was shaken by a sense that the bearded man's self-assured laughter proceeded from obvious certainties to which only he was a stranger. He felt hurt, in his memories, the most defenseless part, and, unable to digest an emotion except through the catharsis of action, cast about for a way of making this clear to the others. A brace of partridge rising from the hill suggested the material for an object-lesson, a form of admonition which had never failed him with his children or his salesmen. "Get them laughing, get them thinking," he quoted, and went up to his room for his gun. In a few moments the party on the verandah saw him emerge onto the lawn, shoulder arms comically, and march off in drill-step singing "Over There." "What's up?" ejaculated Macdermott, interrupting himself briefly to cast a baffled glance at the manufacturer. A fellow-intellectual shrugged. "Good hunting, Mr. Lockman!" trilled an oblivious voice from an upstairs window, serene in its *malentendu*. The rebuke had missed fire; no one had caught his meaning; and, half-puzzled, half-dismayed, Joe, still in march-time, his thin-skinned face knotted in conflict, vanished into the trees.

Up above, in the meadow, flushing the long grasses for game, he came upon Will Taub, still standing on the peak. Joe had no way of knowing that the soul of the realist chieftain was in a delicate condition, *enceinte* with a new man. He had observed him down on the lawn and marked him with a foreman's eye, being as yet too much of a novice in intellectual circles to distinguish conversation as an authorized branch of labor. Idleness actually frightened him; he could not behave normally in its presence. He was tired himself now, though he did not admit it, and the sight of the able-bodied man young enough to be his son (here Joe was mistaken; there was only ten years difference in their ages) taking it easy on the summit brought on in him one of those fits of nervousness that another's inactivity always produced in him. He

felt an impulse, not so much to chide Taub, as
to do something to get him moving. He knew
very well that he ought not to interfere; the
man was a stranger to him—"Remember, you
are not at home," Eva had warned him already;
"don't be too familiar; these people don't know
you, Joe." But the same fatality that made him
drop a pot-lid in the kitchen at seven o'clock in
the morning when he had promised to be quiet
and was moving about on tip-toe overrode him
now. "Just a word to the wise," he said to himself in extenuation. "Come on, Joe, let's get the
lead out of his pants." "State Police reporting,"
he announced in a loud voice, coming up from
behind Taub and shouldering his shotgun playfully. "Work or the guardhouse!"

Taub swung around with a start; his trem-
bling hands jerked up hastily above his shoulders, as if by their own volition, in a gesture out
of Keystone comedy which appeared both ludicrous and utterly natural, as though his whole
life had been an apprehensive preparation for
this summons. He stared woodenly at Joe, his
mouth opening and closing. Joe broke into a
laugh. "Gotcha," he shouted, "brother. Say,

boy, what's wrong with your nerves?" But as Taub's face began to relax, Joe saw from it what he had done. The sympathy he had ready for all sick and wounded creatures commenced at once to flow. "Oh," he said impetuously, "I'm sorry." He put out a hand to touch Taub's shoulder. But he could not modulate to solicitude without a glissade of buffoonery. "Aw," he exclaimed, mock-wheedling, kicking a foot in the dirt in imitation of an urchin, "I didn't really scare ya, did I?" Getting no reply, he grew still more contrite and serious and spoke finally in a natural voice. "Forgive me," he declared with a sigh. All this time, he was studying Taub's face eagerly, hunching his neck and pressing his own unshaven face with the rimless glasses forward, like a woman pleading her cause and searching the features of her lover for some token or clue. The reality of this terror was patent enough, but he was concerned to find the reason behind it. Having injured Taub, he had no wish to think ill of him (contrary to general practice), and the idea that Will was naturally fearful could not therefore enter his mind. A thought finally dawned on him. "Shucks," he exclaimed.

57

"I ought to have known. You're a radical."
Taub nodded dumbly, accepting this, almost
with gratitude, as the most favorable explanation of his conduct. But as soon as it occurred
to him that he *was* after all a radical (the prem-
ise of his career recalling itself like the features of a forgotten friend), a righteous anger
took possession of him. The trampling hooves
of the police horses, the night-sticks flailing
about, tear gas, arrest without warrant, torture,
tar-and-feathers, all the indignities he *might*
have suffered for his beliefs came vividly before
his eyes: for all Joe knew, he had undergone
them in person, and Joe's ignorance now of the
real facts of his history allowed him to think
quite sincerely that this hypothetical case was
his own.

"Ignorance is no excuse!" he yelled suddenly,
turning on Joe and advancing a threatening
step in his large white shoe. "What are you
doing here?" He knew very well that this must
be one of the colonists but chose to act as if no
common tie could connect them—in this way he
imagined that he was freed from the usual sanc-
tions of behavior. Heedless of Joe's expostula-

tions, he brandished a fist in the air and bellowed, "Get out," sternly. "No trespassing," he added, carried away with his thoughts and pointing to an imaginary sign. "This is private property."

Joe's face looked pained. "I guess introductions are in order," he suggested with mild reproof. He was perfectly certain that Taub knew him for a Utopian; Taub's eyes, seeking to avoid an act of recognition, kept sliding insecurely away from a meeting with Joe's face, so that his very violence had an element of constraint and even dissimulation which Joe did not find sympathetic. Nevertheless, to save Taub embarrassment, he presented himself formally. Taub stared at him a moment, and then broke away without answering. He had placed Joe suddenly in his mind and remembered that it was Macdermott who had imposed him on the Utopian council. *"Fools!"* he muttered to himself as he strode off to his cottage. "Why did they bring him here? They must have been *mad* to think of it." All his benignity had vanished; it seemed to him that the apparition of this clown was a part of a plot to deride

59

and humiliate him in some fashion that was still obscure. His whole being felt outraged by what he had just gone through: practical jokes were anathema to him; they belonged to an order of things which defied his powers of anticipation, like children, birds, cows, water, snakes, lightning, Gentiles, and automobiles. The thought of associating with Joe over a period of months struck him as truly preposterous; he felt deeply offended with Macdermott for having taken it for granted that he could.

His mood was somewhat bettered by an encounter with two of the purist children, who, having witnessed the scene on the peak, leapt out at him from behind some bushes, pointing make-believe guns at him and shouting, "State Police." This time, at least he was not taken off his guard. Recognizing a young Macdermott, he tried a genial tone. "Well, little man," he said, appropriating from some long-dead uncle this form of address, "what does your father think of your pointing guns at people?" "My father is a dope," young Macdermott answered promptly, and Taub laughed aloud with pleasure at this echo of his own thoughts. "Ha, ha," he said, "that's good," and he went off toward his cottage rehearsing the child's phrase softly, well pleased with himself and the world. His own question and the boy's answer seemed to him extremely witty: Susan disappointed him, when he stopped to tell her the story, by taking it too matter-of-factly (she had many nieces and nephews). "Poor Macdougal," he elucidated, with a groan of half-genuine sympathy as he set himself in the ideologue's shoes. "What a comedown for a pacifist! His own children call him a dope."

Yet this deathblow, as he felt it, to the pretensions of the Macdermott faction did not quite dispose of the anger evoked by the collision with Joe. He went to bed in a bad humor, having quarreled with his wife about the stove, and was awakened very early by the sound of shots outside. To get back to sleep was impossible. In the city, he would have dressed, gone out tieless onto the street, bought coffee and a paper and felt himself king of the morning, the news, and the sleeping Village. But here he could only toss and wait for the communal breakfast, which was to be served in the central building, at an hour he was powerless to advance. When he came out at last onto the lawn, wearing new work clothes which scratched him and cumbered the freedom of his gait, he found a small commotion. Off to one side in the clearing, Joe was doing target practice at an improvised rifle-range he had created by fixing some tin cans to locust-trees. The young veteran and the news editors had sauntered off to join him; others remained to watch, for the news had already got around that the oil stove was flooded and breakfast would be delayed. A good thirty, however, were gathered in the kitchen, where the cook of the day was sobbing, having burned off her bangs and eyebrows when she put a torch to the stove. She was laughing and crying at the same time, for while she prized her appearance (it was she who had brought the elaborate wardrobe), she had, so it happened, been Joe's sponsor, together with her husband, and, recognizing her protégé's hand in what had just befallen her, she was trying to treat the matter as lightly as possible.

"What happened, Katy?" Taub inquired with real solicitude; an accident to another moved him to identification. "Him?" he conjectured softly, darting a serpentine glance in the direction of the clearing, and nodding his head profoundly as he felt his suspicion confirmed. "Joe?" she answered vaguely. "I suppose. He was trying to get his breakfast without asking anybody anything. I ought to have warned him not to touch the stove." Katy Norell was aware that this forgivingness sat well on her, in lieu at least of eyebrows and hair, and she continued to repeat the explanation of just how it had happened to everyone who entered the room, until what had begun as sincere extenuation became, by asseveration, a kind of unpleasant accusal, since the latecomers would never have connected Joe with the accident if Katy had not told them exactly how he came to do it. Joe's wife, Eva, in fact, tapping forward from the doorway on her small high heels, flung her a bitter look and absorbed herself very pointedly in a study of the stove's mechanism, as if to suggest that the conviction rested on dubious testimony, and that this silent iron witness would tell a different story if it could. Young Preston Norell, observing this, put a cautionary finger

63

on his wife's bare elbow and nodded with his eyes toward Eva. Katy broke off in confusion. "Did my husband do that?" Eva demanded, facing her now directly, with a tone of impeachment. Katy blushed and hesitated. Everyone had turned toward her; there was an expectant silence in the kitchen as the colonists waited to see how this first crisis would be met. It was not a friendly atmosphere but one of suspended commitment. "Watch this!" said Taub's eyes prophetically to Susan; at the door, someone hushed a member who demanded to know what was happening. The interest, for the spectators, centered on Katy's character. With anyone else, it would have been a simple matter to say No or Yes and make an end of it, but the struggle she was having to pronounce a ready disclaimer was visible even through the soot on her expressive features. She did not dare to say Yes, though this was what nature urged on her, and she feared that a strong No would imply a previous lie. "It was only an accident," she said finally, in a feeble and unveracious voice. "Somebody was careless and left the oil turned up without lighting the stove."

64

Preston Norell's long fingers dropped from his wife's arm, and he pushed his way out in disgust. For those words, *only* and *somebody*, he wished her in hell; he was sick and tired of a wife who could not bear to have people believe that she had flooded a stove which in fact she had not flooded. "Who cares!" he exclaimed aloud in a veritable frenzy of boredom. Katy's vanity he did not object to; indeed, he found it entertaining, but the irresolute repetitiousness of her character, the perpetual see-saw between intention and execution, illustrated so banally in this incident, reminded him of his mother, a well-meaning woman whom he disliked. This produced in him the disagreeable sensation of having been born married, though in fact he had celebrated his second wedding anniversary only a few days before. A nomadic and restless temperament, he had felt a deep-going antipathy to Utopia and the suggestions of finality it conveyed: Katy had teased and persuaded— they must go and live for others, she insisted, in the same tone of pretty conviction with which she demonstrated the absolute necessity of a new dress or an apartment which his salary

65

could not afford. As usual, he had allowed himself to be reconciled to a commitment which bound him more tightly—the freedom stressed in the manifesto seemed to him a very ethereal entity compared to the freedom of movement he renounced when they entered the gates. Now, the *contretemps* about the stove, the querulous morning mood of the colonists, the failure of breakfast to materialize, the lack of sportsmanship of his wife, combined to bring on an attack of the most violent claustrophobia—he struck off across the lawn, going he knew not where. His fury was out of all proportion to the cause that had provoked it; he had left his wallet in their cottage; he was dressed in shorts and sneakers; his job was gone and his apartment sublet to a war-worker: in an hour he might relent, but the need to be *elsewhere* was stronger than common sense. Someone called after him, but he paid no attention; the other colonists and the environs were included in his anger with Katy; he thought of Utopia simply as a place in which it would be impossible ever to escape from her, a multiplication of marriage or its projection into eternity.

66

She was following him out now; he could hear her footsteps running behind him; she caught him just beyond the lawn, her face distorted with tears, which he could envision with perfect distinctness while keeping his eyes averted. "Forgive me," she cried. "Forgive me!" Plainly, she was not going to pretend, as she sometimes did, not to know how she had offended; the others were watching curiously, and he perceived, with a certain savage satisfaction, that she felt she must deflect him from whatever course he was planning, before their rupture was public. "Go in and get the breakfast," he said sternly, shaking his arm free. "Pull yourself together. You disgust me."

Her sobs instantly grew louder, and he threatened her with his eyes. Her condition awoke no pity in him; he had seen it too often before; at the same time, a certain politic instinct cautioned him not to drive her to a point where she could no longer control herself, for suddenly he was not sure how he wished this quarrel to end. Arrested in his trajectory he became conscious of the practical difficulties of leaving, and the humiliation she would suffer if he should do so moved him to compunction. Feeling nothing but distaste for her as she stood there before him, he nevertheless foresaw a state in which she would be pitiable, poor derelict thing, just as he remembered, without any particular interest, a moment when she had been lovable, only the night before. At bottom, he felt responsible for her, and it was the very strength of this feeling that made him detest her now. He remained silent therefore and waited for her sobs to cease, fixing her with a schoolmaster frown and tapping his foot impatiently. "Go back," he commanded at length, when her breath began to come more easily. "If *you* will," she stipulated childishly, but at the very suggestion of bargaining, all his hatred revived. "No," he said, shaking his head rapidly several times, the blond hair gleaming in the sun. "Go." "But you'll come soon?" she persevered. He shrugged his shoulders in half-concession; he would promise nothing verbally.

Katy started to walk slowly across the lawn. Having secured from Preston what she interpreted correctly as a guaranty of return, she began to consider the quarrel in quite a different light, to ask herself, first what account she should give of it to the other colonists, and, secondly, what apologies and admissions she could wring from him later in the day. The phrase, "You disgust me," kept surging up to her oesophagus like something she had been forced to swallow but could not assimilate; if it were not retracted, she felt it would literally kill her. At the same time, she was aware of the folly of reopening the discussion; her husband, rearoused, was only too likely to repeat it. That this phrase might embody an actual truth of feeling elicited from her consciousness only a vague and irrelevant wonder: is it possible, she asked herself in a tone of disinterested curiosity, that he does not love me? And though she was in the habit of cross-examining him tenderly on this point ("Do you love me?"—"Yes," "Perhaps," "What do *you* think?"), she found, to her surprise, that the possibility of a negative answer did not really exist for her. "Nonsense," she said to herself, "he *must* love me," and the notion that he perhaps did not simply annoyed her with him, like some idle, neurotic fancy or an over-conscientious scruple. A nicety of feeling which could withdraw him from her in spirit, while he remained physically on the premises, exasperated, even as a hypothesis, everything practical and quotidian in her tenacious and self-centered character. "I would not forgive him for that," she declared to herself precisely, forgetting that the offense she postulated placed him by definition beyond the reach of her disapproval. But the instant this difficulty became clear to her, and the psychic absence of her beloved appeared suddenly as real, as real as the death she feared for him whenever he left her side, the armies of her love rushed after him, to surrender and bring him back captive. To surrender and treat afterwards was Katy's habitual strategy in love, but now, shaken by her husband's words, by the presence of on-lookers, by the fright she had just given herself, she made a great resolution: to resign herself to his condemnation as to an immutable fact of nature, to take it, that is, seriously. For a single moment, in the severe northern light, darkened by the long shadows on the mountains, she had a perception of life as a black chain of conse-quence, in which nothing was lost, forgot, forgiven, redeemed, in which the past was permanent and the present slipping away from her (contrary to her instinctive opinion, which was that the past could be altered and actions, like words, "taken back"). She nearly cried out with pain as this unconscionable truth bit into her, and she recognized that the events of the past half-hour were, literally, irrecoverable. Such powerlessness, guilt, and desolation she had known only in nightmares, and from those she had, naturally, awakened, a fact which had misled her into considering evil a dream. Here for the first time, this impulsive and ingenuous nature found itself alone in a cold and unresponsive climate in which to announce, "I have ruined your morning," did not constitute a refutation of the truth that indeed she had.

Accustomed to please, to smile, and court, and be petted, she felt the sensation of having given displeasure to forty-odd people as something so alien that she could hardly connect herself with it. That this had "had" to happen on the very first morning, when she, more than any of them, had wanted things to go well, she could only attribute to the malignant perversity of circumstance, and the pathos of the distance between her hopes and the reality received its final nuance when she presented herself in the kitchen, ready to take over, and found herself superseded, her menu set aside, and Eleanor Macdermott and Irene, the girl student, hurriedly making eggs and toast with silent, starched faces, as if in the presence of illness. With that instinctive tactlessness so common among educated people, they made no remark on her absence but simply became more busy. Lacking any fresh impetus she wandered vaguely over to where her big bowl of waffle batter stood untouched, like a pariah, precisely as she left it, except that the table around it had been very carefully wiped. "Would you like me to put it in the icebox?" Irene inquired, kindly, but with a manner decidedly mortuary, which suggested that this object revived associations too painful to be borne at the moment. Katy picked up the enamel spoon, which had been washed and aligned beside it, with that same hint of obsequies and ritual observance. "It's too late?" she hazarded timidly, and the girl looked at her and sadly shrugged. She had studied Greek with Katy, and the humiliation of her teacher was painful for her to witness. "Much too late," put in Mrs. Macdermott firmly. "They're sitting down inside." "Come," said the girl gently, taking the spoon from her hand. "Come and eat." Katy shook her head; her large brown eyes filled with tears. "I can't face them," she muttered.

"Nonsense," said the girl maternally. "It was not your fault, you know," and indeed such was the impression that prevailed among the majority of the colonists, who believed that Preston had stamped off blaming her, unfairly, for the accident and the late breakfast, while a dissenting minority on the other hand, could not be swayed from its verdict, which was that she had flooded the stove herself and had been caught by her husband trying to pass the buck to Joe. The code of honor articulate in the colony was by no means so theatrical as Preston's: Macdougal Macdermott, for example, would have given a great hoot of laughter if anyone had proposed that his Eleanor "confess" to an oversight not her own—"For God's sake, Preston, come out of it, man; you're living in the Middle Ages!" The marital quarrels of the Norells, moreover, were too regular a feature of this society to excite any great curiosity, since everyone but the participants knew what the outcome would be. Only the young minister, with whom self-questioning was a vocational aptitude, could have wound his sinuous way through this labyrinth of error and triviality, and he had a priest's tolerance—Katy's capacity for regrets, together with her classical studies, had convinced him that she possessed a genuinely religious nature (ethics, in his view, had little in common with religion; every third Sabbath he produced a sensation in his rural flock by calling on the ladies of the altar guild and the Girls' Friendly Society to abandon the specious assurance of salvation by works).

Katy, at any rate, allowed herself to be persuaded and made her appearance in the dining room, with a mournful step that suggested the whole chorus of *The Suppliants*. A picture of grief, silent, composed, unassuageable, had suddenly proposed itself to her imagination, and the sincerity of her inner feelings passed off at once into performance, as she bargained on the power of this *pietà* to move her husband to pity. But when her ranging eye at length discovered him sitting at the far end of a long table, wedged in between two other colonists, his high-colored face averted and obdurate, her heart collapsed within her. These moods of his (she recalled) could last as long as a day, and she felt really quite unequal to the tedious process of reconciliation which, in view of the fact that she was sorry, seemed to her highly unnecessary, like some legal routine or the difficulty of getting passports. Her interest in expiation quickly vanished in the face of its actuality. She could not be bothered with it—"It is simply too stupid," she thought, experiencing on her own behalf that rational impatience with suffering that made her detest cruelty, injustice, poverty and wars. Men, to Katy's mind, were born to love one another, and their refusal to do so she attributed to that same mulish obstinacy which her husband was demonstrating here in the fraternal hall. A strong will and a weak character had led her greatly to over-estimate the plasticity of the human material, and indeed that of matter itself: she recognized no obstacle to the general attainment of plenty and happiness, just as she saw no reason why she should not have a new Plato or a hat.

Preston now, no doubt about it, was taking advantage of the Utopian brotherhood to shut her out from himself. In this, she felt something unsportsmanly and even illegitimate: he knew very well that here, before all these people, she was helpless to secure his attention, and he must know also how she would suffer if he were to go out to the fields and leave her, without so much as a look. That the privacy to make a scene was something she would miss in Utopia was a contingency she had never anticipated, but now, surrounded by these watchers, she felt deprived of a basic right, the right to go over and expostulate with him, behave badly if necessary, until he responded to her grief. Preston, on his side, was discovering in the Utopian situation a privacy he had sought in vain during two years of marriage. Though unaware of his wife's exact location, he presumed that she had come into the room, but he had no intention of speaking to her until much later in the day. He felt protected by the others, in precisely the manner she assumed, and a cruel streak in his character was rejoiced by this turning of the tables, this illustration of poetic justice: little had she thought, when urging on him the manifold blessings of Utopia, that *this* would prove to be the chief. At the same time, however, he was conscious of a purer happiness, an extraordinary sense of solitude, as though he walked on a carpet of pine needles; the conversation around him acted as a kind of blanket which muffled the din of relationships; he sat alone among others, peacefully absorbed in his thoughts. As if on an ocean liner, a train, or a crowded foreign square, he recaptured his identity in a nothingness, an absence of the acting self. He was recalled to this world by the scraping of chairs in the dining room. The men were setting out for the fields.

Outside, on the porch, a vast elation seized him as he considered the empty morning and the loneliness of the work ahead. It had rained during the night, and the sky, still tossed with clouds, and the rumpled mountain landscape had an air of exhausted wildness, like a face on which the tears have just dried. This comparison, which came to him wittily, evoked the figure of his wife, who had strangely slipped from his mind, and, suddenly well-disposed and merry, he rushed into the kitchen to find her, whirled her twice around the room, and let go of her, to the discomfiture of Eleanor Macdermott, whose sense of permanent ill-feeling toward this *femme savante* had been somewhat mollified by the suspicion that she was about to become an object for charity. Katy, surprised and delighted, smiled her pleasure at once; she had never learned how to stay angry, which was perhaps a defect in her character. Yet the terms of the amnesty were too vague to set her mind altogether at rest, and forgetful of that resolve, which had seemed only an hour before essential to her moral survival, she detained him at the screen door. "Preston," she ventured. He turned and waited politely, certain of what was coming but unwilling, even now, to please her, except on his own terms. "Preston!" she repeated. He raised his eyebrows in a look of inquiry. She did not know what to say. "Do I really disgust you?" she whispered, looking nervously behind her in the direction of Eleanor Macdermott. "Yes!" he cried emphatically, but with a shout of laughter; the conspiratorial manner of the question struck him as splendidly farcical—in his very tenderest moments, he looked upon Katy as a comedian. He now relented and patted her sharply on the buttocks. Katy returned to her work, in some peculiar fashion well pleased; though she had broken her resolution and come off with nothing to show for it, it seemed to her undeniable that she had acted for the best.

Meanwhile, *sotto voce,* in another part of the dining room, the realists were earnestly conferring. A tap on the shoulder and a significant nod of the eyes had directed each member of the faction to the small table at the rear, where Taub, spooning the dregs of his coffee, measured with a brief glance the loyalty of each newcomer and invited him to pull up a chair. Susan Hapgood was present, Harold Sidney (Will's oldest and most cautious ally), John Aloysius Brown, Danny Furnas, Fearon Powers, and several others; the wives had not been included. Taub had already narrated his experience of the night before, and for the benefit of the late arrivals, Harold Sidney kept furnishing a rapid whispered summary of the outrage, like a respectful usher at the door of a meeting. Exclamations of indignation were general—"I think it's just *terrible*," Susan Hapgood cried, each time the story was told, her small-town capacity for being scandalized asserting itself somewhat ingenuously in this new sphere. "Don't you, John, don't you, Fearon?" she asked, turning her pretty birdlike brown head in sudden alarm and indecision to every member of the party. "Yes, yes indeed, quite," they reassured her. The problem was, what was to be done. Taub, who had been waiting imperturbably for this question, like a headliner idling in the wings, proceeded to unfold his plan. Any board member, he pointed out, had the right to call an emergency council meeting, without stating his reason, if eight hours' notice was given. Council members, therefore, would be notified immediately of a session to be held that night, *in camera*, at his cottage, to act against an unnamed person who had been guilty of asocial behavior. This procedure would give Joe's friends neither time nor occasion to organize a counter-movement on his behalf; the atmosphere of mystery would demoralize any potential opposition, which would waste and scatter its energies trying to guess who was meant. "Bad conscience," he explained stonily, regarding his confederates with a look almost of warning. "That's how we get these moralists. Make each one think it's *him*." He gave a brief snort of pure laughter. "And don't give them a chance to discuss it." "Why not at five o'clock, then?" asked someone, counting on his fingers. The realist leader frowningly shook his head: conditions of secrecy were indispensable; happily, they could infer from Lockman's hour of rising that he went to bed early. "What if he has insomnia?" put in Brown, with the air of a veritable Aquinas and laughing heartily at the same time to indicate the savor of the jest. He was a philosophy teacher who had been converted from Marxism to the absurd, an ungainly and aggrieved man full of insistencies, who imagined that his jokes were not understood. "I say, Will, what if he has insomnia?" he repeated, flapping a loose forefinger to command Taub's attention. Taub shrugged impatiently; he did not greatly care for Brown, whom he considered too unstable to be of much use in practical affairs. "Insomnia gosomnia," he remarked, dismissing the objection.

"At ten o'clock at Will's, then?" persisted Harold. He had feared and honored Taub too many years not to feel that a great importance attached to having the meeting take place in the chieftain's living-room, in the shade, so to speak, of his numen. "The team always plays better in its home park, eh, Will?" he queried, nudging Taub and giggling. Taub acquiesced with a grin and, seeing his audience receptive, was moved to recall a time when control of a committee had been, as he put it, "stolen" from him by a fellow-member who on the pretext of economy had simply removed the offices to his own apartment. "That taught me a lesson," declared he, with a reminiscent groan, and his male associates ruminatively nodded their large heads in concord, amplifying the thought. "What about the Macdermotts?" objected Susan, who felt slightly chilled and alienated by this elephantine strategy. "They will want to stay home with their children," she explained. Taub and Sidney, thunderstruck, exchanged a consultative stare: Macdermott's three children, they were agreeing, constituted a real political asset; how many meetings, on their account, could not be transferred to Taub's quarters?

Little Furnas now spoke up to remind them that his wife was assistant to a pediatrician, a detail which they had also forgotten. "Helen will be glad to stay with the kids," this youngest realist promised. He too, like Susan, was observing in himself certain doubts about the validity of this kind of procedure, being also a "creative" writer and hence more sensitive to morals. But his temperament, more equable than Susan's, was not very long disquieted: he felt sure that it made no difference whose house the meeting was held in; Joe Lockman had rather appealed to him as a type of Chassidic simpleton; he took only a perfunctory interest in Taub's grievance and its airing. A pale, fat, blond boy with humorous, good-natured, round eyes, he remained in the Taub faction principally from laziness and from a novelist's feeling for plot. Taub, for his part, looked on him with paternal indulgence; the "discovery" of new talents formed one of his chief relaxations, and he never foresaw the moment when the child would walk unassisted.

Following Furnas's offer, the realists hastily dispersed, assuming nonchalant expressions and mingling with the other colonists as though to assure the community that no division of purpose was contemplated and that the conference just ended had been merely a social reunion. In the barn, where partnerships were forming and work-stations being assigned, Powers and Taub and Brown promptly chose partners who were not identified with their faction, put intelligent questions about farm machinery, prophesied rain or drought, according to their temperaments, joshed with the purist women— in their effort to appear unconstrained and matey, they avoided not only each other, but even the eyes of their wives. The purist leaders, for their part, also strove for a natural demeanor. Certain that something was afoot, they did not wish to show alarm or curiosity. They felt that the good of the community now depended on their ability to keep their heads. They had not long to wait; as they separated to go to the fields, they were detained, one by one, by the discreet cough of Harold Sidney, who drew them aside to "wonder" apologetically whether they would be free to drop in at Will's after supper. To Sidney's surprise, everyone seemed to know who was meant by the "asocial person" and to take it quite for granted that a meeting should be called to discuss him. Somebody must have talked, he said to himself grumpily, and his thoughts lit on Susan Hapgood with a little sting of satisfaction—Taub told her too much, as he himself had often hinted in the past.

But Sidney was mistaken; no one knew of Taub's adventure. The conviction that Joe did not belong here had, in less than twenty-four hours, obtruded itself on all but the most unobservant as an obvious, inescapable fact; and the purist leaders, who had been dreading an attack from the realists on quite another front, now felt positively light-hearted to think that it was *only* Joe who was in question, and did not stop to inquire what charges the realists could be bringing, once Harold's face betrayed to them that their guess had been correct.

They did not condemn the business man;

85

they looked on him as on an erg or a dyne misplaced in the human family. But misplaced he certainly was; the point was a delicate one, and they were aware of inward relief that, thanks to the realists, they would not be put in the position of being the first to raise it. A weight had been shifted from the individual conscience to the deliberative powers of the council as a whole, and the very colonists who had been asking themselves most anxiously how Joe should be dealt with now suddenly stopped thinking about the matter and referred the problem of curbing his energies to the consensus of opinion. Macdougal Macdermott, skirmishing with a last doubt, linked arms companionably with Harold Sidney, as they started up to the forest, and put to him the question that bothered him, just as if this veteran enemy, who fell obediently into step beside him, were in reality an old comrade-at-arms. "How about it, Harold?" he urged, in a tone already hesitant and conceding. "Wouldn't it be better to ask him to come and talk it over with us himself? More open and above-board?" Sidney shook his head sadly but firmly. A clever and fair-minded man, receptive to discussion and argument, he disliked giving pain, and this, in conjunction with the doctrine of necessity to which he and his colleagues were wedded, had made him somewhat weak and evasive. With his wispy grey hair and grey mustaches, loose clothes and unsettled neck ties, he gave an impression of middle-class goodwill submitting helplessly to *force majeure*, an impression which was only misleading if one failed to recognize that this relentless law to which he reluctantly yielded was simply the code of self-protection and the desire to have an easy life. Thus, unlike Taub, he appeared always open to conviction, while anchored to unchanging beliefs. His flexible mind extended to take in his opponent's position and then snapped back like an elastic, with the illusion that it had covered ground.

"I agree with you," he was saying to Macdermott. "On the surface, it looks like a raw deal. The man's out of his depth here; that's the main point. I recognize that." It was a peculiarity of Harold's speech that a certain trick of melodic division, of phrasing in the musical sense, gave his remarks a stilted and unnatural character which he tried hard to remedy by an "easy" and colloquial diction. The result was that he created an effect of speciousness, even when he was most in earnest. "Now take the actual situation," he continued. "We call him in for a discussion. He gets sore. What do we do? You know yourself what people are."

Mac did not press the point; he still felt unsure in his own mind what attitude he ought to take to the capitalist and hoped to thrash one out in the course of the evening's debate. He was never quite certain what he thought about anything until he had tested his opinion for seaworthiness in the course of some polemical storm. His own objections to Joe had rested wholly on pacifist grounds. The sound of gunfire upset him, yet he was far from positive that his uneasiness had a theoretic justification. The taking of human life was not at issue in target-practice (except, of course, by accident), and to cite the danger of accidents was to avoid the nub of the difficulty. People were killed every day by reapers, stoves, falls in the bathroom, and many good things had been used for bad ends—oil, steel, coal, human beings themselves. Was it the gun as such that he opposed or its utilization in warfare and murder? If the gun, then he opposed hunting, and in that case he ought, by logic, to oppose the slaughter of domestic animals. Here, however, Mac had baulked. It had often been said of him by his adversaries, that he would end in vegetarianism, and though of late years he had been admitting with a good deal of combative energy, "Yes, of course, I'm a crank, a crank like Thoreau and Gandhi!" the identification of himself with these distinguished predecessors betrayed his real view of the label. He did not hold eccentric views gladly; he felt that they were imposed on him by the inexorable clarity of his intelligence, but he was firmly resolved *not* to take the last step, to resist vegetarianism to the end, whatever temptations it offered him, as though by belying the prophecy he could prove his intellectual freedom and set destiny at naught. Now, it was with something of the emotions of Oedipus on hearing the shepherd's tale that he had found himself, on this fine spring morning, brought, by the process of his own reasoning, to the brink of fulfilling the words of those ideological oracles who were determined to type him, resist and splutter as he would.

In his relief at finding that others, and not pacifists either, felt the same way as he did about gunfire (what else could Sidney be alluding to?), he let the subject lapse into a comfortable disorder. An antipathy to firearms, he supposed, went pretty deep in human nature—there was no need, really, to push it any further. Time enough, he promised himself, to argue procedure at the meeting and work out a formula for action consistent with respect for the individual. The warm sun, the sound of the axes in the forest, where clearing was already beginning, the small flask of wine in his pocket made him feel sportive and friendly. He clapped Harold on the back, confident that he had misjudged him in the real world down below where the pressures of society distorted natural relations; and they worked side by side all morning, the editor taking his cue from the man of practicality, who was an expert woodsman, like many city intellectuals who retain, in the midst of cynicism, this single link with boyhood. "Burying the hatchet, eh?" Taub remarked with a genial lift of his eyebrows, as he came upon them together somewhat later in the morning; his corns had begun to hurt him, down below in the kitchen garden, where he had been put to work following the plough with a lime-bag and sweetening the newly turned soil. *From each according to his capacities* was the cardinal principle of the colony, in labor as well as in morals, and Taub, acting on this injunction, had readily subcontracted his task to the girl student, who had been standing at the end of a furrow, watching him with lively, amused grey eyes. He had spent so many years in executive positions that it seemed to him quite fitting that someone younger than himself, and less powerful in a worldly sense, should take over whatever was onerous in the work of the day. The sense that he had other, more important duties to attend to persisted with him here, and quite naturally so, since he had persuaded himself of this truth once and for all by referring the importance from the duties to himself. It was, in fact, with the genuine feeling of conferring a favor that he passed the heavy bag on to Irene and went off to his cottage to soak his feet, emerging shortly afterwards to prowl about the property with a preoccupied and restless air, stopping here and there to check up appreciatively on the progress of the various enterprises ("Hard at work, eh, Preston?"), note the formation of partnerships, and the labor potential of his friends. And there was in his behavior something so natural, so apparently instinctual, as though he had been a lynx obeying the order of its kind, to roam in unsurfeited watchfulness while others did their slumberous toil, that no one grudged him this leisure, not even Joe, who, after the previous evening, had felt a protective concern for him, and this morning, from time to time, would wipe the sweat from his brow and anxiously shade his eyes, to pick out the ubiquitous Taub wherever he might be on the property, pacing up and down with his soft, creaking step, or flung weightily at last into the hammock, his hands folded over his belly.

Had Taub been informed of Joe's kindly feelings toward him, it would have had no effect on the determination he brought that night to the meeting. An expression of esteem from a person he was bent on destroying only increased his contempt and inflamed his punitive fervor by removing the fear of reprisals. Incorruptible in vengeance, he could not be swayed, either, by pity, which he looked on as a form of bribery offered to the softer emotions. Money and fame also were incapable of deflecting his anger, for these attributes became loathsome to him when he saw them in "the wrong hands." It irritated him to be quietly reminded, as he was repeatedly during the course of the day, by members of the council, and even by his own wife, that the colony was being run through contributions, on a wholly voluntary basis. He himself had contributed nothing to the enterprise, beyond a small down-payment on his cottage, not because he was miserly (he was capable, in fact, of large-handedness), but because, very curiously, he was physically unable to do so. Many times, at the preliminary council meetings, his hand had reached for his pocketbook and stopped, as if seized by a stranger. His reluctance to be committed held him aloof financially, and the more conscious he grew of the dubiousness of not having given (hearing the treasurer report that a school-teacher had donated her life-savings), the more he could not give, lest he seem, by making things right, to confess to a previous remissness. The allusions to Joe's money and generosity infuriated his vanity, and the implication that he, as a realist, did not know his own interests came as the last straw. Receiving his advisors after supper for coffee and a last-minute briefing (no drinks were to be served, as if to mark the unfriendliness of the occasion) he suddenly lost control of himself when Danny Furnas, blinking, asked him whether he had considered the colony's treasury sufficiently. "Money!" he declared contemptuously. "That's all you can think about. Macdermott's sucker!" he cried, his face darkening and swelling with those viscous emotions which rose to his brain like blood clots whenever he was ascribing to some person more scrupulous than himself an act of baseness or venality. "You're all alike!" he proclaimed, hammering on the table and grinding his teeth together, as though bodily possessed by the Lowest Common Denominator.

Danny's milk-blue eyes grew wide and innocent. Looking around at his fellows, he appeared to estimate the truth of this charge. It saved trouble, he found, to treat all statements as if they were meant literally. He nodded thoughtfully twice, pursing his full lips, to indicate that on the whole he was compelled to agree with Taub. Taub, deflected, stared grumpily at his colleagues.

There was little discussion, after this, between them: they sat leafing through magazines and tinkering with the portable victrola; Macdermott, Sidney reported, would vote with them, and Eleanor also, presumably. This, to his faction's bewilderment, seemed to make Taub only more moody. He grunted, almost with displeasure, as Harold undertook to show him that his group was in the majority. "Never mind that. Who's against us?" he demanded, with a slow resuscitation of interest, when the Norells, possibly Haines, and Desmond, the Catholic scholar, were ticked off, one by one, in Harold's methodical style. "A-a-h, we'll vote them down!" he spat out, suddenly brisk and businesslike, heaving himself forward in his chair and quailing his followers with a look.

From the outset, there had been a clear under-
standing that the will of the majority was not
to be used to coerce a minority, though no actual veto-power had been written into the by-
laws, the colonists concluding, from the lesson
of historical events, that the veto-power itself in
the hands of a stubborn minority could be an
instrument of force. Danny Furnas now raised
his blond eyebrows into semi-circles of questioning and made a whistling motion with his
lips. Not being a sentimentalist, he saw no need
for a display of theoretic virtue; his vote would
speak for itself. Meanwhile, though mildly, he
interposed a new demurrer. "They may resign,
Will," he pointed out, wondering whether he
could frighten Taub by the prospect of a colony
without workers. "Nah!" said Taub, defini-
tively. "They won't resign. Where would they
go?"

Danny pushed forward a judicious lower lip
and gently rocked his head back and forth, as
if considering. "M-m-mm," he finally conceded,
and let his chin sink to rest in his palm, using
an elbow for a prop, in the attitude of a philo-
sophic student at a lecture that promises to be

endless. This disengaged and contemplative position he retained throughout the meeting; his chin gradually sank deeper into his palm, till only the broad short nose and musing round eyes were visible. The most popular of the realist faction, he was the recipient of many bipartisan winks and nods, as the other council members came rapidly through the door, more prompt in attendance than in the city and peculiarly more self-conscious. Curt greetings were exchanged; Desmond cocked a jewel-like green eye at the coffee-table and registered the absence of the whisky bottle; he and Editor Haines passed a wordless message of comment; the secretary opened his notebook; Eleanor Macdermott cleared her throat.

"You have the floor," she declared drily, convening the meeting and gesturing to Taub to begin. The group turned toward him expectantly, shifting their camp chairs. A feeling that the present meeting would serve as a test of strength had suddenly become a certainty to nearly everyone in the room. How, nobody could imagine, so that a little stir of curiosity quickened, not altogether displeasurably, the insistent sense of foreboding that the inclusion of the realists in the experiment had attached to every action and gesture. Conscious of this suspense, and prolonging it for tactical reasons, Taub sent a shrewd, probing look around the room, appeared to estimate for a moment, nodded curtly to himself, took a draught of his cigarette, exhaled slowly and luxuriously, opened his mouth to speak, and suddenly found himself wordless. In all his arrangements and calculations, he had overlooked only one thing: what he wished, concretely, to propose. The expulsion of Joe Lockman had figured only hazily in his mind as the possible outcome of his intrigues, and he had imagined proceeding toward this blur by a series of easy stages. Certain harsh scenes from later in the evening, it is true, his own clenched fist and protruding thumb raised on high to demolish the unavailing argument of an opponent, Macdermott's weak, angry stammer, Katy's frightened eyes, had appeared to him with a vivid distinctness that enslaved his powers of attention and left him no freedom of thought. Awaking abruptly from their spell, seeing all these faces directed toward him clad in Sunday democratic expressions, he did not know how to begin: his habitual fear of showing his hand too early made him utterly incapable of an initiative. After a moment of baffled reflection, in which his intelligence struggled to give quasi-judicial form to the mass of spiteful feelings which had suddenly ceased to seethe in him, he contrived to find a way out. "I'll pass it to Harold," he announced, in a bland and matter-of-fact voice that took no notice of the general amazement or of Harold's irrepressible start. He leaned abruptly back, audience-fashion in his chair, his arm flung loosely to one side, waiting, as it appeared, to hear Harold's thoughts on this subject, quite as if they were not as familiar to him as his own. Sidney, rapidly running over the agenda as he understood it, found himself also at a loss. He did not know what Taub wanted him to say, and was obliged, finally, to lean over to consult him in a whisper. Taub frowned at his suggestion and emphatically shook his head. Harold shrugged and threw up his hands despairingly. Taub tapped him and whispered; Sidney concurred, doubtfully, and after a last-minute flurry of indecision, got up and began to speak.

"I assume," he commenced jerkily, with an aborted 'easiness' of delivery, "that we're all friends here. What I'm going to say reflects no criticism on anybody present. We all make mistakes . . ." A few perfunctory nods acknowledged this preamble; he went on in a more businesslike tone. "Suppose we start with last night . . ." And he began to rehearse, very much in the manner of an attorney representing a client in a damage suit, the story of Taub's experience on the mountain-top; the effect on his nerves and sensibility; the traumatic shock he underwent when he imagined himself arrested by a policeman ("Cossacks we used to call them —you can all remember that"); Taub's radical background; his alienation as an intellectual from the mass-culture of the drugstore and the radio serial. He then went on to describe Joe— a well-intentioned Babbitt, a Boy Scout still living in the escapades of the First War, a useful citizen perhaps, but unfitted for an environment of neurosis. Finally, the broader impact of Joe on the community: the target-practice; broken sleep; the danger to the children; the stove (admittedly an accident); Katy's hair; her quarrel (if he was not being too personal) with her husband. He looked to Taub for further directives and, receiving none, sat down.

"The question!" cried Katy. "The question!" She had come prepared for a battle, and could not refrain from pressing her advantage.

Sidney looked at Taub and both shrugged their shoulders. There was a short silence. Sidney coughed deferentially. "I think Mac has something to say." "Well," said Mac, rising to his feet, "I *did* have a few things on my mind, but you boys . . ." and suddenly he began waving his arms as if in an uncontrollable fit and laughing, a high, flute-like sound interspersed with patches of helpless choking. "Oh, my God!" he cried. "Will!" Danny Furnas looked up and began to snicker also. In a moment, the room was convulsed. Harold's giggle soon could be heard, Haines' deep, husky guffaw, and finally Will's chuckle, beginning unwillingly and gradually mellowing, as a large foolish smile wreathed his irresolute features in a look of the utmost contentment, in which vanity, chagrin, and relief were indeterminately distributed. His cumbrous thighs spread apart, tightening his ill-fitting duck trousers at the crotch, his bare arms hanging at his sides, his polo-shirt gaping at the neck, he presented a boyish picture of a proud and gratified culprit; the real ingenuousness of his nature sprang into sudden prominence. This man of transparent secrets, caught, as it were red-handed, yielded himself pleasurably to the boisterous humor of his companions, like a small-town kid dragged struggling from his place of concealment during a game of hide-and-go-seek. Only his wife, Cynthia, was immune to the general merriment; she looked coldly down her straight nose at her fellow-Utopians, until she was quite certain that this was all in fun. Her ideas were rather rigid, like those of a royal duchess. She had a firm sense of her husband's position, and she wished to be assured that there was nothing seditious in this laughter before giving it countenance.

"And Harold!" Macdougal cried, when he was able to articulate. "That speech!" He laughed again until the tears ran, yet appreciatively, without pettiness, as though paying tribute to a genuine though unconscious work of art. "A great ambulance-chaser was lost in you," he declared, almost seriously, shaking his red head, and taking Harold by the arm to indicate the kindliness of his feelings. This risibility of Macdermott's was the crowning and unexpected grace of his character; it was an *élan vital,* seemingly springing from nowhere, which buoyed him up and translated him into a realm of pure essences, beyond the pedantry of judgment. The targets of his satire could never truly dislike Macdermott, for they found themselves endowed by it with a larger and more fabulous life. Taub and Sidney, now, could not but feel that this laughter left them somehow in an improved position; it reconciled them, to their surprise, with themselves and with others, and permitted them to live down a humiliation whose causes they were reluctant to search for in the duller chambers of blame and excuse.

Sensible of the change in the atmosphere, Taub retired to the kitchen and came out with whisky and glasses. Someone went to the main house for ice and soda water; Preston Norell fetched wine, and the treasurer took the opportunity to draw Taub aside and ask him for a contribution, a thing he might well have done earlier, had not something ungenerous and straitlaced in his goodness (he was a member of the purist faction) been unwilling to help Taub to extricate himself from a false position. "You should have asked me before, Henry," Taub remonstrated softly, as he got out his check-book and in his large, unformed handwriting, scrawled out a medium-sized check. Henry, a tall, thin young man with an ovoid head who resembled a nail-file, felt an immediate rising of irritation; his pride as a functionary was nettled at having negligence ascribed to him when he had merely not exceeded his duty; at the same time, his conscience admitted that the reproof was, in a finer sense, justified. But that he should be made to seem guilty, twice over, once wrongly, once rightly, while Taub remained blandly innocent, infuriated this radical young printer, who was not accustomed to dealing with persons of a certain eminence. He took the wet check, blew on it, and withdrew to a corner of the room, rebuffing a whisky and soda. "Thanks, my wife and I don't drink," he declared.

That evening, nevertheless, marked the beginning of the lyrical phase of the community. The issue of Joe Lockman was allowed to drop, once Editor Haines had contributed "a very sensible suggestion": that Joe should be requested to hold off the shooting till after breakfast-time. "Do you want that in the form of a motion?" Eleanor Macdermott asked. "No," everyone cried. "Just let someone speak to him," and the secretary closed his book without having taken a note, since no official business had been transacted. Later, sitting on the floor, a little apart from the others, Macdermott and John Desmond tried to analyze what had happened to the realist case. "It's a fundamental weakness of their position," Macdermott was explaining in a low voice, as if he were passing on a war-secret. "They don't know what they want. Give them the floor and they'll hang themselves; I've seen it every time." Desmond, who was very handsome, nodded with a somber face. "Revolutionary nihilism," he muttered; he was sufficiently new to his recaptured religion to refer every phenomenon to a pronouncement of the Church. "Those boys aren't revolutionists," Macdermott whispered scoffingly. "They're conservatives. They're so conservative they're afraid of their own thoughts." Desmond listened doubtfully, with an evasive hitch of his fine, square shoulders. "The terms need defining," he declared at last, very softly and thoughtfully. Macdermott coughed. In general, he enjoyed speaking with people who disagreed with him or people less intelligent than himself, but now, still full of his subject, he was in want of a congenial listener. He got up, excusing himself, and went over to Taub, who was standing smoking alone by the fireplace. "Why not Taub?" he said to himself simply. "Say, Will," he announced, raising a half-playful finger, "I've got an idea for you . . ." And he began to explain to Taub, quite without malice and indeed with the desire to be helpful, just how he and his faction always defeated themselves. Taub listened with interest, nodding slowly as he took in the argument, and moving his lips slightly, repeating Macdermott's words under his breath, as if storing them for the winter. "You're all wrong, Mac," he placidly declared, when he saw that Macdermott had finished. "What?" demanded Mac-dermott, unable to believe his ears, and beginning to gasp and stutter. "Is that all you have to say?" He felt utterly nonplussed and bewildered, like a suitor rejected without an explanation. Taub gave a confirming nod, and then, with great exactness, crossed two large fingers, held them aloft for attention, and then, having secured Mac's eye, repeated, with the measured delivery of one who is speaking for history, "You're all *wrong.*"

This was the last open combat to take place between the two leaders. Both emerged from it with a sense of victory, and a sense, also, of wasted time. From then on, discussions between them dealt only with practical matters or with neutral subjects from which no positional inferences need be drawn. Hopeless each of persuading the other or of dealing a blow which, from the point of view of the receiver, could be recognized as incapacitating, they resigned themselves to their differences and commenced, for want of anything better, to see each other's good points. A burst of friendship followed this easing of relations, as often happens in love-affairs when two people decide that they do not "mean much" to each other. The practical gain in sociability, in evening-calls, work-sharing, advice offered and taken, was immense. Yet there was no doubt, as the more alert purists began to notice, that the *idea* of the colony had somehow received a setback. The hope of establishing a Universal to which all men would pay homage was being tacitly set aside in favor of a policy of live-and-let-live. The discovery that one cannot convince an opponent and that it is hopeless to go on trying involves a confession of subjectivity that deprives the world of meaning: the colony, it seemed to the Norells and Leo Raphael, a poet, was losing its *raison d'être*, if it was no longer a question of converting Taub and his faction to a manifest Truth but simply of getting along with them on a day-to-day basis. Was it really worth while, they asked themselves, to have come all this distance, and invested so much ardor and energy, only to produce what was, in effect, another summer-vacation colony, cooperatively financed? For the regeneration of a soul, a nation, a party, according to the feelings of this group, admission of past error was requisite. The Nuremberg trials and the de-nazification proceedings had demonstrated, a few years before, that it was impossible to *impose* an awareness of guilt on a man who declines to feel guilty, yet now they could not help but feel a baffled thirst for justice as they watched Taub and his cohorts complacently settle down in Utopia, as though it were their natural preserve.

For while there was perceptible in the realists the dawn of an ethical attitude, a certain subordination of self to the requirements of the general welfare, an idea, at worst, that here they were answerable for their deeds to someone and not simply to an historical process, which condemned nothing but failure, these symptoms of improvement were unaccompanied by any revision of their official preconceptions or their general outlook on life. These remained intact and indeed untouchable. The happiness they were experiencing during all this month of June, they refused to take into account in formulating a social theory; while turning an old butter-churn or milking a cow by hand, they continued to make the statement that you can't turn the clock back, as though this postulate were unshakable. Once the colony had won their approval, they began to treat the enterprise as an exceptional case, a weird freak of circumstance which could not be repeated under any other conditions. Nothing, they insisted, was proved by what was happening here: the weather had been favorable, the personnel carefully chosen; the hotel and its mountain vistas an incomparably lucky find. No lesson, therefore, could be learned here which would have a general application; and in fact the more smoothly the tenor of life began to run, the more they dismissed the colony as being false to the total picture. The ordinary man, they maintained, was incapable of revising his habits to the extent that they themselves were doing, though only a few months before they had maintained the same thing about intellectuals.

In their refusal to admit that anything was being demonstrated by the experiment, something more than a quibble was involved. There was an aspect of this multiple virtuousness that they found precarious and unsettling. As the days flowed on, and the corn grew in the fields, the hay was got in on time and the cows and the chickens were producing, they became more and more conscious of a sense of unreality, as if they were in a dream or behaving atypically in public. *The experience of the age* was a phrase to conjure with in their circles; and whatever could be alleged against them, they felt secure at least in their period-authenticity. Now, since the moment of their arrival in Utopia, they had felt cut off from their era, in a very curious way. The wholesomeness of the Utopian life, the success that was rewarding their efforts, the vast scale of the scenery, the good impulses they felt, all seemed to them to lack what they called relevance, to be out of date, like a tone poem or the verse of the Lake minstrels. And so, while responsive to these experiences, they continued to hold them at a certain distance, as if they were not *for them*. When they said, therefore, that the Utopian lesson had no larger validity, they meant that there was a part of themselves which Utopia did not touch; boredom and urban cynicism had become so natural to them that an experience from which these qualities were absent seemed to be, in some way, defective.

As the month passed, however, connections with the world were resumed. Visitors came and went; Utopia was written up in the newspapers. A photographer came from *Life*, and, smiling into the camera, even the doubters experienced that sense of naïve verification that the inexperienced traveler feels when he buys a picture postcard of his hotel and inscribes an x by his room. A hand-press was quickly imported; they had decided to publish a magazine. The work in the fields went on, but since they were not growing for the market, the total labor required from each person amounted to only five hours a day. In the evenings, in the big lounge, by the oil lamps, they began to have lectures and readings from the poets and philosophers. A scene from Molière was put on. The clergyman held services on Sundays, which were attended mainly out of curiosity. A waterfall was discovered in the forest, and they swam in the pool at its foot, with Taub like a chthonic deity looking on from a rock in his shorts. Bicycles were bought; they went on picnics in the neighborhood. The women made bread and cakes; Susan Hapgood had a birthday. They found watercress in the brook, tangled with the pale forget-me-nots. The first young lettuces were eaten, and cauldrons of mustard-greens boiled. And, like a pocket mirror held up at a distance reflecting their own husbandry, far off, across the valley, the fields of the remote farmer altered with the advancing season, but so swiftly that it seemed as if overnight contrasting strips of pale green were laid down, like lengths of carpet on the mountainside, supplanting the dun-brown, and supplanted in turn by lemon-yellows, then golds, then brown again, as a clover-crop was turned under or a field of mustard harvested.

In the real world, the war still held off: a letter arrived from Monteverdi—he was alive but in hiding. "The only hope," he wrote them, "is in small insurgent communities, peripheral movements . . ." Katy Norell wept, with shining St. Joan eyes, as the letter was read aloud on the verandah by Francis, the minister, and the realists averted their glance but maintained a respectful attitude, like unbelievers in a church.

"Oh, dear, we haven't done *enough!*" cried Katy desperately, when it was finished, banging her knuckles on a table and confronting them all with this self-indictment. It seemed to her that Monteverdi relied on them to spread the message abroad, and that they had failed him by becoming merely self-subsistent; the others, however saddened or thoughtful, felt no impulse to join her in a *Domine non sum dignus* which, for all its sincerity, had so clearly personal a reference; she was comparing herself, with all her shortcomings and weaknesses, to the great work the letter suggested to her. She wept because *she* was not perfect. "I don't know, Katy," answered Susan, easily. "It seems to me we've done mighty well."

An unsettled relation existed between these two learned women, in which there was a good deal of rational accord without sympathy. Monteverdi's letter had not excited Susan, except in so far as it contained good news of himself; his remarks about small groups, peripheral action, et cetera, she found rather unimpressive—naturally, he would put faith in such movements; why not; he was an anarchist. A distrust of libertarian doctrines had stuck with her from her Marxist days. Over a period of years, she had watched her friends, one by one, having made the break from Marxism, plunge with exhilaration into Proudhon and Tolstoy, but her normally curious nature felt no inclination to share an experience so uncorseted. "That side" of the colony made her intelligence squirm, and her silence was a protest which, in her opinion, should have acted as a constraint on others, but which did not at all seem to do so, so that she felt obligated from time to time to put in an official disclaimer, when she really should have preferred——or so she daily assured herself—— to bracket the matter altogether. She thought that it should have been plain enough to Katy and her associates that she, rather violently, did not wish to "go in" for Monteverdi's ideas, lest they destroy her liking for him—he himself, in former days, when they used to meet in company, had shown a greater delicacy and seemed, by his shyness, almost to co-operate in her reluctance to having exposed to her the contents of his mind. Susan's small-town courtesy prompted her to ignore, even in private, what did not bear thinking about. She read Tolstoy, of course, but a certain virginal decorum preserved her from his ideas. "I look on him primarily as a novelist," she would demur when someone tried to wring from her at least an awareness of his message. Exercising what she considered to be the same charity on behalf of her friends, she strove not to acquaint herself with the details of their enthusiasm, to speak of it, when necessary as a stage which they would outgrow, or a species of mental illness from which they might recover. Indeed, she hoped that by ignoring it she could make this "phase" pass, and resented the unawareness of the Monteverdians which seemed, on its side, to take no account of her abstentions. "Why, that sounds kind of *religious* to me," she would reply uncomfortably if obliged to listen to Katy's translations of the Founder's thought; so her own aunt had spoken, doubtfully shaking her head and laying down her sewing, when Susan brought up arguments in favor of racial equality—"Sounds kind of communistic . . ." Thus the purists' persistence and the native shrewdness and precaution which made her look anxiously on ideas as something one could catch by contagion had kept her for some time from thinking at all about political questions which she left now to Taub, whom she considered her intellectual superior, though she disagreed with him sharply in everything that mattered to her most. To Katy, a natural proselytizer readily infected with enthusiasms, Susan's unwillingness to change masters was a source of continual disappointment. That Susan could remain unmoved by a call so clearly heard by herself, drove her to a teacher's despair, and her habit of incessant comparison led her at once to inquire whether Susan was not more admirable, for being less facile in feeling, than she was. Anything short of perfect communion depressed Katy, and Susan's way of taking everything that she said literally, without the liberality that interprets and supplies feeling-tone made her imagine herself misunderstood and discovered simultaneously; and it was true enough, as a matter of fact, that Susan did not greatly care for Katy while giving her precisely her due.

Other letters besides Monteverdi's began to come from Europe. The manifestos of the colony had apparently been circulating through the yet-unoccupied countries, and from all sorts of persons, mostly poor, middle-aged, and obscure, requests for information, for literature, and above all, for passage-money arrived. Leo Raphael, reading these, charmed by the strange locutions and the naïveté of the demands, began to conceive a vast plan for a peace-fleet, to be financed by the United States Government, that would carry away from Europe all those who rejected for themselves a totalitarian way of life and who yet were unwilling to risk the terrible cost to humanity of another war for democracy. He saw a poetic vision of a continent left empty before the advancing invader—the silent factories, and houses, the anti-aircraft guns, the museums, waiting like a shell to frustrate the will of the victor, who would find on hand to receive him only those who welcomed his tyranny. This version of the scorched-earth policy had also, as he pointed out at a general meeting held on the Fourth of July in the dining room, the merit of practicality. It would be actually cheaper for the United States to send over empty ships to bring back the peace-loving passengers than to send, as it was doing, steel, planes, bombs, guns, to governments which were, in many cases, too timorous and unstable to use them, or to send wheat, corn, and fats to keep alive populations whose life-expectancy, clearly, was a matter of weeks or months. "The armaments we are now shipping will simply fall into the hands of the enemy. If we must feed democratic Europe, it is cheaper to do it here. If we must fight, we will do it here, also supposing that we are invaded. *They* ask us to divide the world with them in a policy that is called appeasement. Let us agree to do this, but only in a geographical sense. Let them keep the geography of their hemisphere and we will take the populations. Canada," he continued, warming, "will clearly be willing to co-operate. Already in the last war, there was talk of moving the British Government to Ottawa. We will establish socialism," he went on, as the implications of his thought became fuller, and his dark eyes lit up with a fanatic love for the beautiful; he saw the American continent from Alaska to the Straits of Magellan, blue, white, golden, productive, inhabited by all the nations, each speaking its own tongue and cultivating its own gardens, the Italians in the California vineyards, the French in the moist valley of the St. Lawrence, the English on the ranches of Wyoming and in the councils of Washington and Ottawa, the Spaniards in Peru and Mexico . . . "Socialism," he explained, "will be a necessity. The task cannot be accomplished without it. We will create an internal market in an economy of abundance. This will be the new imperialism, full production for peace."

He drew a deep breath.

"This country," he continued, more quietly, "has one tradition that is viable. It has been from the earliest times a haven of refuge from tyranny. The Puritans in New England, the Catholics in Maryland, the Irish peasants oppressed by the landlords, the victims of '48, Russian Jews fleeing military service, the refugees from Mussolini and Hitler." Harold Sidney coughed. "What is this, Leo, a Fourth of July speech?" he demanded with a self-conscious laugh. "Sssh," put in Susan, peremptorily, "I want to hear what he has to say."

"All our messianic wars," Leo explained,

realizing that the word *imperialism* and the citations from American history were having a misleading effect, "have been fiascos. We have mistaken our role. We cannot carry democracy abroad with military expeditions or food shipments. We can only receive it here, when it comes to us looking for entrance. America is ideally a harbor, a state of the utmost receptivity. It is not our role to lead, but to be open. America, I imagine, if this plan can be put into effect, will disappear, at least as we know it. America is only a vessel, waiting to be filled, a preparation for something that has not yet happened. That is what we all have been sensing in the air, ever since we were children, a restless, bemused expectancy of an event that will come to stay with us, like a visitor. I remember," he went on, "those summer afternoons on a lake in New Jersey, with a still haze floating over everything and a phonograph playing somewhere, and a row boat drifting in the water, as if time itself were pausing, just on the edge of the incredible. I express myself very badly," he interpolated, slipping into a more ordinary voice.

"Never mind your autobiography, Leo," called Macdermott, laughing. "We get you. Go on. What do you propose?"

"That should be clear," said Leo. "I propose a United States of Europe, to be constituted in the Western Hemisphere, with a system of joint government by all the member nations. A United States of Europe in Exile, to be made up, not of politicians, but of ordinary people and intellectuals. I leave the details to you," he added, winking broadly, and sat down.

"Supposing they don't want to come, Leo?" insinuated John Aloysius Brown, with such an affected air of smiling and subtle scholasticism, that no one paid any heed to what was really a sensible objection.

"Hear, hear!" shouted Joe, silencing him and jumping dynamically from his seat. Everything half-articulate in himself, his humanitarian feeling, his Americanism, his Jewish sense of the melting-pot, his respect at the same time for a variety of cultures, with each man worshipping his own gods without interference, he saw suddenly clothed in glory by the poet's gift of expression. The tears stood in his eyes as he considered the beauty and simplicity of this idea and the lives it might have saved if someone had only thought of it sooner. "You've got a great business head, my boy," he declared. "Bring the consumer to the goods, that's telling 'em." His admiration for Leo's plan paid full tribute to its practicality, but this implied no derogation of its idealistic intent. "The internal market," he repeated, wonderingly. "That does it!" "Think of the housing developments," someone else put in, half-seriously. But Joe was not joking. "Yes," he said, nodding thoughtfully. "There's a billion dollars' worth of business right there." He felt as though this were the moment that had been promised him from the instant he first heard of Utopia and perhaps from the instant of his birth. His day of fulfilment had come, and if he himself, like Moses, were never to see the Land of Promise, he at any rate tonight had glimpsed it from this mountain-top, like Moses on the mountain of Nebo. In all his weeks in the colony, this was the first truly Utopian suggestion he had heard.

"Not bad," said Taub, concedingly, when the business man went to press him for his opinion;

they had been friends for nearly three weeks. "Not *bad?*" cried Joe. "What are you talking about? It's great." Taub protruded his full lower lip, reflecting. "An interesting propaganda scheme," he admitted. "Propaganda!" Joe demanded, unbelievingly, his grey face paling and contracting, as though with a physical pain. He made a short aggressive movement toward Taub, and Susan believed for a second he would strike him. "It's something to work *toward,*" she explained, in a soothing voice. "No congressman would ever vote for such a thing," she elucidated. "You know how *shamefully* they acted about the DPs."

"Pressure," said Joe. "Promotion. Private enterprise could help." He turned the idea over in his mind. "Business is pretty backward," he twinkled an eye at his audience, "but we're the boys that get things done." He turned suddenly to Leo, who had begun to move about restlessly, like a performer who feels out of his element, now that the show is over. "There was a little too much socialism in that talk of yours," he remonstrated playfully. "Listen to the old fogey," he added, raising his hand to his mouth, in a vaudeville stage-whisper to Eva. Eva bridled. She had been having a wretched time here. Her plump little sybaritic feet had been swollen from almost the first day; she had caught poison-ivy all along her white arms, still smooth and womanly at fifty; her fingernails had cracked from the hard water; she detested a double bed; but more painful still than these afflictions, was the sense that her husband was making a holy show of himself before all these younger people. Having no interest whatever in the arts, though she did not object to piano music, she nevertheless, felt that she knew how to comport herself in an artistic atmosphere, a conviction of authority which she had derived principally from the movies and magazine-reading. Artists, she knew, were sensitive people who surrounded themselves with beautiful things, and the sensitiveness of her pampered little body, her love of material comfort, she took as evidence that she herself possessed a latently artistic temperament. She saw nothing in the behavior of the Utopians to confirm her preconceptions, yet the fact that quite frequently in the public rooms she heard conversations she could not understand overawed her to the extent that she felt mistrustful for Joe, whom she considered as ignorant as herself and far less dexterous in concealing it. "If he would only be quiet," she ejaculated in an undertone to the minister's wife, who was the only person she felt wholly in accord with. "He'll pay for this tonight," she promised, with a sigh, and for a moment her well-preserved face held a hint of the furies, though the retribution she had in store for him was simply a digestive disturbance, the result of too much excitement. "He pays for it every time," she added. There was an appropriateness, seized though not fully analyzed by Eva, in the fact that Joe's body, which he refused to coddle, should prove to be her ally, and her allusions to its behavior suggested a wealth of knowledge more intimate and exclusive than love.

"Private enterprise?" Leo inquired, his alert head tilted to one side as if he were listening for a new music that might be drawn from these old syllables. He had the virtues of gravity and sweetness, accompanied by a nimbleness of mind that found inspiration in the most commonplace remarks. "Well, Joe," he said, "let's see," and he linked arms companionably with the older man, prepared for a long discussion. At the same time, there was something merry and quizzical in his face which admonished his listener that conversation was an art. "Privateering?" he speculated. "That, too, is in the tradition." And very rapidly he sketched out a plan for a covey of small frigates, manned by individual enterprise, to conduct rescue raids on the European coast. "If we get the co-operation of the State Department (and you're quite right, business can do it) we land the passengers in New York Harbor. If not," he waved his hands airily, "there are other places in the Americas." And his mercurial fancy, working supplely with historical materials, at once created a new image in which the War of 1812, the old slave raids on the African coast, the secret rearmament of Palestine, Henry Ford's peace ship, the exploits of smugglers and pirates, caves, dark inlets, rowboats with muffled oars, furnished a solid mass of precedent shot through with the gold of romance. Joe once again was charmed, but the doubt implanted by Taub

127

caused him, after a moment of contemplation, to look up suddenly at Leo with a frown and catarrhal sniff of suspicion. "Is this on the level?" he said.

"You think it's not practical, Joe?" Leo answered him, almost tenderly, a light caress in his voice. "You think it can't be done. I recognize your objection. It must be the oldest in history. You remember the story of Columbus. And there was Archimedes and the airplane. And Dunkerque, you remember, was described as a military impossibility. Every daring invention . . ." He paused to smile faintly. "Sex, surely, must have been the first. What a ludicrous action if looked at from a rational standpoint. Many of the philosophers complained of it."

Joe motioned him to stop. He was a modest man and there were ladies present; moreover, the asceticism of his nature inclined him to agree with the philosophers—like many virile business leaders, he was sexually recessive. "You've proved your point," he said. "All right, let's get busy." The other colonists turned toward him. Many of them had been moved by

Leo's first proposal to feel a fresh stirring of political hope. The second proposal they had dismissed as merely fanciful, and in fact even the most visionary of them, the Norells, the Macdermotts and Nelly Boardman, the woman illustrator, who was drunk, suspected that about the whole evening there hung an element of japery, for they knew Leo well enough to recognize that there was nothing dogged or persistent in him. He was not earthbound like themselves; he parted easily from a notion when it proved inconstant and often grew bored with his theories when someone else tried to unite him to them in a marriage of practice. This opinion of his political seriousness, naturally, was held even more emphatically by the realist group.

Yet, despite this, and despite a certain discomfort which his readiness in oratory induced in them (the joke about sex was self-plagiarized), an altruistic fervor in the colony was kindled by what he had said. Most of the Utopians, no matter how selfish, had been in the habit of working at least part-time on behalf of others, whether as teachers, as editors, or as simple entertainers; even Taub considered that he had

had an educative function to perform in the world down below. They had supposed that their altruism would have full play in the co-operative work of the colony and in the example they would set to the world, but the truth was that, having identified themselves whole-heart-edly with the enterprise, they had lost the sensation of sharing, and hence it seemed to many of them that their life here on the mountain-top was almost too hedonistic, since they were enjoying a happiness which had be-come an end in itself. Their withdrawal from the world had appeared legitimate, when a war which they could neither avert nor dominate threatened Western civilization, but now that the war held off they began to pose once again the question of alternatives, and to ask them-selves whether this haven, which they had so readily constructed for themselves, could not in some manner be enlarged until a retreat from war became indeed a counter-attack upon it.

Leo's plan seemed as good as another. It was at least a starting-point and each man in his own mind quickly began to modify it to suit his own notion of the possible. Macdermott, in one part of the room, was proposing a pamphlet to set forth Leo's ideas to the small public of intellectuals whose names he retained in his files. Jim Haines envisioned an open letter to his former publisher—short, terse, factual, to be illustrated by a huge balance sheet comparing the cost of Operation Peace (as he provisionally titled it) with Operation War. Susan imagined a campaign of letters and telegrams to Senators and Representatives. Ed Jackson suggested a hook-up with the World Federalist people. Taub wondered whether the idea could not be grafted onto the mind of some prominent personality (a journalese term that had become dear to him). Desmond thought of a diocesan letter; Danny Furnas, of working with the trade unions. The capture of a college president indicated itself naturally to several, and the radio announcer kept jumping up and offering to return to the air under their sponsorship.

But when a roll call was ordered to distribute the work of these proposals, an enormous number of practical obstacles to doing anything whatever suddenly made themselves felt. There was a rush of volunteers for typing, mailing and filing, but the originators of the key suggestions began, one by one, to find reasons why their ideas were unworkable. Haines, with a certain shambling embarrassment, got up to explain that the Open Letter, on which everyone had, above all, been relying, would require the help of a research-girl, not to mention a financial expert: he did not have the Marshall Plan figures here or the details of our military loans; the shipping costs would have to be calculated, and the fees of the technical advisors— in short, he had been too hasty. Mac's pamphlet, he suggested, would be much more to the point. Katy Norell, when called upon, had an abrupt recollection of certain uncomfortable interviews in the office of her college president; she could write to him, she supposed, she said doubtfully, but surely there was someone else who would be able to approach him more easily. Ed Jackson was obliged to admit that his connection with the World Federalists was rather tenuous; it might be better, on second thought, to try the United Nations. Susan still declared herself ready to compose a letter to her Congressman, but unfortunately she had forgotten his name. Danny Furnas knew the names of several of the younger trade union chiefs; they, however, did not know his. "You're pretty thick with those boys, Jim; maybe you could help me out." Jim Haines' dark rumbling voice spoke easily. "Can't say as I am, Danny." Everyone in the room became instantly certain that he was lying. Desmond, who had buried his fine head in his hands, savagely, as if wrestling with his demon, suddenly looked up. "I would be glad," he murmured politely, but with an air of Irish *hauteur* and coldness, "if anyone wishes it, to drop a short note to the *Commonweal*." The secretary scribbled briefly in his book, but the immediate proposals in hand, when the roll call was finished, had shrunk to a single suggestion, which it was within their own power to accomplish; that Mac should get out a pamphlet, with the help of Henry and Preston, outlining Leo's plan. There was a painful silence. No one, not even Mac himself or Eleanor, had any real confidence in the efficacy of this idea. How many pamphlets, remarked Preston, had not Mac got out in the past, with the sole result, as far as he could see, that the dining room he now stood in contained fifty not-very-charming people. "Perhaps the pamphlet will influence *us*," he drily suggested.

"Why not drop the whole idea?" asked John Aloysius Brown, rather maliciously. "We're too cut *off* up here." Taub, seeing the way the wind was blowing by the noncommittal and evasive faces, promptly withdrew into his shelter. "Better call it off," he decreed. But the Macdermotts felt immediately offended at the implications of this advice, though it accorded with their own inner weariness as they saw themselves once again confronted with the unwieldy machinery of the world as-it-was-constituted which had worn out their youth and patience as side by side, with so little assistance, they had struggled in vain for leverage. It was as if Leo's plan, by appearing so deceptively simple and natural, had led them back into the old impasse and abandoned them to their own devices. Yet the suggestion that they were unimportant and powerless, they would not accept from another. "Too small for you, eh, Will?" Mac demanded. But as he looked around him his pugnacity quickly deserted him. He felt old and tired.

"Well, of course," he said sadly, "If nobody wants it . . ."

Katy and Susan, in unison, cried out vehemently in reprobation. "We do," they insisted, covered with shame for themselves and for the company at large. Their sudden loss of energy had been the result of a collective awakening from a day-dream. For a short half hour, everything had seemed so easy. People had appeared to them infinitely malleable, simply the instruments of their plan. The Congressman in Susan's consciousness had had no need of a name; he existed in a vacuum equipped only with a desk, at which to open the letter which he had been conjured up to read. Katy's college president had been simply a rubbery outline which she could stretch to her measure. And any doubts she had experienced as to her ability to do this in practice had been lulled to rest by her confidence in the influence which would be exerted by others, as though all the public figures and prominent "personalities" would yield compliantly together to the ardent temperature of the meeting, like wax melting in the sun. When the stab of Haines' defection had pierced this joint assurance, reality had all at once by contrast assumed a character infinitely hard, impermeable, and the Congressman, for example, from being a nothing, a receptacle, became an entity so resistive that to obtain his name from a newspaper became a task that seemed to Susan for the moment a veritable labor of Hercules. But now that the faint-heartedness of the membership had reached really scandalous proportions, their feminine sense of propriety rallied them to indignation. "I thought we were all agreed," began Katy in her classroom manner, "that Leo's idea had merit." She paused for rhetorical effect and when no one contradicted her, continued with a sarcastic precision which she had learned from her old Latin teacher, and which sat like an antique hat on her impetuous and still-girlish delivery. "In that case, we might do it the honor of working for it ourselves." Here she carefully directed her gaze away from the vicinity of Jim Haines, for whom, as a matter of fact, she was busy constructing excuses, as for some favorite male student who was inexplicably delinquent in his work. To Katy's mind, Jim Haines figured as the pivotal member of the community; he represented the normal, and the others turned anxiously around him, like the satellites of a sun-king. Though he seemed unaware of this pre-eminence or too-boyishly reticent to take notice of it, the fact was that nearly all the members had set themselves out to please him, not because he had been more successful than themselves in the world down below, but because, with his deteriorating resemblance to an Arrow Collar ad, his moody air of dissipation and long-limbed Lincolnesque melancholy, his shambling gait and diction, he typified the middling sensual man of democratic persuasions to whom the appeal of Utopia was beseechingly addressed. Everyone considered it a miracle that he was here among them, full of domestic habits and the know-how of the ax and the monkey-wrench, the eternal father of the family, busy with small repairs, hospitable with the whisky and soda, large-minded and impatient of women, whom he treated with ceremonious gallantry. And though there was some vague speculation as to what exactly could have persuaded him to make this hegira with them, on

137

the whole it was felt that this was one of those things that it was better not to inquire into too closely, lest analysis "vanish" him from their company, like Cupid under Psyche's taper. Operation Peace, as first sketched out by him, had seemed an almost incredible bonanza, and the group, when disappointed of it, had done its best not to appear crestfallen and to act as if what had happened had proceeded not from a man's will or the lack of it but from some irreproachable natural order—it had been really too much to hope for, Katy and Susan had murmurously agreed.

"It's silly," Katy went on, resuming her ordinary demeanor, "to try to interest other people in this plan when we've done nothing for it ourselves. We have to begin with the pamphlet and reach as many readers as we can. Then . . ." she gestured vaguely, "we will see what can be done. I was just talking to Francis." The young minister gave a nod of acknowledgment, slightly rising from his seat; he was extremely conscious of his holy orders and showed a great sensitivity to quotation, as if he were an authorized text. "He suggests that perhaps

138

the next step would be to form an organization, something like the old CARE, to bring people here instead of sending them packages."

"That is substantially correct," said Francis, with a short clerical clearing of the throat. "Naturally, we would begin in a very small way. The advantage is that such a practical fund, by enlisting people's charitable impulses, would expose them to our idea, and also lead them, before very long, to look for a way of financing it at the public expense." He coughed, and the meeting, after a second of incomprehension, burst into laughter and applause. Francis' sermonizing voice, nature's gift, apparently, he played on for profane effects that seemed sometimes almost blasphemous; many a sardonic epigram uncoiled itself guilefully in his periods like the serpent in the garden of innocence. The more naïve Utopians hardly knew what to make of him; they looked to a leader before laughing at his witticisms as the unaccustomed churchgoer awaits the direction of the choir before venturing to rise for the anthem or seat himself for the sermon in his pew. "He tickles me," confided Taub to his wife, illustrating this

139

remark with a vast delighted wriggle and a poke in the ribs. His amazed admiration had known no bounds from the moment he formed the idea that the decorous young clergyman was an unbeliever of the deepest dye. Had he seen Francis in his room on his knees praying to be forgiven for levity, he would merely have given the young man credit for an artistry more consummate than that which he had already conceded him.

Francis's suggestion, now, combining the Machiavellian with the humanitarian, made an immediate appeal to his fancy. He did not think it really practical; he looked in fact upon the man of God's sense of policy as a kind of hot-house produce of the ecclesiastical atmosphere, too rarefied for this world. Still, he saw no harm in supporting him, provisionally, at any rate. Ever since his break with the Movement, his imagination had been seeking a vision of some tremendous social change, involving the up-rooting of millions, on which to disport itself. The irrigation of deserts, the leveling of mountains, the control of rain and snow, heat and humidity, and, above all, the remoulding of the human material itself, the disruption of ancient patterns—such dreams of power and mastery, far more than its fraternal aspect, were what had attracted him to communism, and his disillusionment with the Movement had sprung largely from its concentration on narrowly nationalistic aims and its abandonment of an insurgent ideology. This imagination of his was too graphic for war to fill the bill for it; he groaned as he heard a fancied bomb land and shrank from the jet-projectile. Not since the opening of the Moscow subway had an event of large dimensions moved him to creative identification, and now, increasingly, as he observed the needle of the meeting swing slowly back to Leo, he felt himself more and more attracted by the very grandiosity of the plan. "Stranger things have happened," he remarked with solemnity to Harold, and his mind, like a great derrick, began moving the peoples of the earth, out of their old folkways and into a new dynamic. "For this we would need atomic energy," he declared softly, after a few moments of calculation. "It is always so in history. The problem and the solution come at the same time."

On this note of tentative willingness the

meeting broke up. Joe Lockman, who had absented himself during the final discussion, appeared in the doorway to summon them for a fireworks display, which, through the offices of a novelty wholesaler in Quincy, he had been arranging for the past week. It had grown completely dark. The younger children were roused from their cots in an improvised dormitory; the older children were called from the lounge, where, with that peculiar lack of initiative characteristic of the dawn of life, they had been playing their eternal game of cards—everyone gathered on the lawn or on the deep verandah, which went nearly three-quarters of the way around the hotel and widened, facing the mountains, to form a kind of jutting deck. Into the limitless night the rockets and Roman candles were launched in a magical colored procession of fountains, sprays, constellations, arcs, spirals, lone brilliant stars cutting a great swath through the heavens and dropping uncompanioned into darkness. On the lawn, the huge maples could be seen outlined in the flashes of light, their gnarled, ancient, peaceable shapes assuming a baroque and terrible aspect. Joe,

142

having hastily quitted his post at the urging of Haines and Jackson, was sketching on the verandah with the help of a pair of flashlights held stiffly before him by Susan in the attitude of an acolyte with tapers. Whistler's *Nocturne* had inspired him to improve on it; he was attempting to trace the myriad paths of the rockets as though to grasp the secret of movement, but depressed by the slowness of his pencil, he flung it down in despair. The air was cold and damp; some of the youngest children began to whimper; others were admonished by their mothers to pay attention to the show. The display itself began to fizzle out, like the promise of the rockets in the sky. The bursts of stars came more sparsely; the same types began to recur—the novelty wholesaler was only human and the poverty of his resources was soon manifest, particularly to the children, whose criticisms were hastily shushed. That sense of longing for the infinite, of regret, and a certain dispiritedness produced by all mechanical marvels, commenced to be generally felt; half-ashamedly, the colonists were wishing themselves in their warm, protected beds. Yet the

143

last golden-white spray as it spent itself for-
lornly in the void evoked a sigh of disappointment. "I could have watched that for ever,"
they assured Joe as they parted.

Taub woke up the next morning in a singu-
larly good mood. A strawberry picnic was
planned for noon in the high meadow. A holi-
day had been declared from the fields, and the
company was to spend the morning in the
woods picking the small wild strawberries, and
then converge at twelve on the meadow, where
they grew in the greatest abundance, and with
the sun-warmed flavor of wine. A prize would
be awarded to the person with the fullest basket.
The discovery of these little berries had been
an event of the richest significance to Taub.
He recalled having gathered such berries with
his mother in the dark forests of the Carpa-
thians, and his first instinctive reaction had
been one of startled unbelief when one of the
children had come running into the kitchen,
where he was meditatively drying the dishes,
with the news that there were strawberries in
the woods. "Impossible!" he had exclaimed to

Susan, but he had gone out to see for himself, and confronted with the tiny, half-ripe fruit, he had stood agog with the coincidence, turning a berry over and over doubtfully in his big fingers, like a jeweler appraising a diamond. The minuteness of the fruit and its rarity, together with the memory of himself, small and uniquely valued by the guardian presence of his mother, had struck him with awe and reverence. He felt his character soften and an unwonted tenderness invade him, as tactfully and even piously he wrapped the little fruit in his handkerchief to take home and show to his wife. A sense of restored continuity soothed his locative anxiety; Utopia appeared as the sequel to a story begun in his childhood, and the fact, which he slowly ascertained after many surreptitious woodland strolls, that the colony not only had these wild strawberries but had them in a greater plenitude than he had ever known in his homeland topped off nostalgic sentiment with the creamy self-satisfaction of the well-pleased entrepreneur.

The season being a tardy one, the fruit had reached its peak on this Fourth of July week-end. It had not rained for some days, so that the kitchen garden needed no weeding, and the berries were in perfect condition. In the main kitchen, Katy and Eleanor Macdermott were frying great pans full of chicken, and Nelly Boardman, the illustrator, was preparing a freezer of vanilla ice cream for Haines and the young veteran to crank. Taub and Cynthia, with their basket, set off rather late to the forest, arms interlinked, and leaning slightly on one another, with an air of mutual solicitude, like a fond elderly couple who have supported life's trials together. The strawberries had drawn them closer; for Cynthia, too, they held memories of a lost idyllic period when, during a summer at Fontainebleau as a young lady, she would eat *fraises des bois* on a Sunday in an upper dining room of Lapérouse and dream of the career ahead of her in the great world of fashion. The Taubs' disparate reminiscences fructified each other and revived the romance between them—the consciousness of social difference which had attracted them to each other had become somewhat blurred by their years of association. Cynthia was estimating, more for her husband's pleasure than her own, what a serving of these berries would cost at a fashionable restaurant today (presuming, of course, that one could get them), and Taub's flat black eyes bulged naïvely at the figures she mentioned; an ejaculation of pain escaped him as if from the region of his pocketbook. Neither husband nor wife was a good picker; they bent arduously from the waist. A sense of their joint dignity would not permit them to squat—and their eyes were too nearsighted to distinguish the round, serrated strawberry leaf from the pointed wild blackberry. Nevertheless, they were content, though the bottom of their basket was barely covered and Taub had begun to think that whatever price could be charged for them would result in a loss to the picker. Halfway through the morning they sat down to rest and idly listened for bird calls, in which Cynthia was instructing her husband. Thus it happened that they heard, quite close to them, the sound of an automobile motor.

This noise startled them both; they had no way of accounting for it. The cars belonging to the colonists were jacked up in a shed; once every fortnight an oil truck made its way down the rutted drive, but no other vehicles were expected, and the drive, in any case, was more than the distance of the meadow from the place in the pine-trees where they sat. They listened for some moments but did not hear it again, and they had almost come to the conclusion that perhaps they had been mistaken when they heard a man's voice, speaking quite near them and in a gruff accent they did not recognize. With a quickening alarm that was not altogether rational, they struggled to their feet, and Taub, parting the underbrush, peered through into the meadow. In a moment, with his finger to his lips, be beckoned to Cynthia to join him, and looking through the opening he indicated, she saw a strange trio, a man, a woman, and a child. Just beyond them, in the meadow, was parked an old car, and, as Taub and Cynthia watched, the three got out pails, the man assigned stations to the others, and they began to pick, very rapidly, like experts who knew the terrain.

Will's first impulse, and also his second, was to return to the big house for help. Cynthia dissented in an undertone, puckering her eyebrows disdainfully; there were times when her husband's caution moved her to a just impatience. "Say something to them," she urged, but Taub shook his head angrily, and a look of conjugal fury flashed from his narrowed eyes. "Then I will," she announced, hoping to shame him into action, but Taub had already left her, and, seeing nothing else for it, being a precisian of her word, Cynthia stepped into the meadow, and addressed the strangers in her thinnest and politest voice. "I beg your pardon," she said. The child looked briefly up, but the man and woman went on picking, without a sign of having heard her. "I beg your pardon," she repeated more distinctly, but again no one responded and not knowing what to say further, her spine stiffening with terror, she drew back into the woods as noiselessly as possible, and as soon as the bushes closed behind her, trotted breathily, teetering on her high heels, back to the main house, where Will had only just preceded her.

Katy Norell, on the verandah, was questioning Taub's story with a troubled face. Cynthia recounted what had happened to her, and Katy listened incredulously; Eleanor Macdermott came out from the kitchen to lend a semi-official ear. "They couldn't have heard you, Cynthia," Katy declared with positiveness. "No one would behave that way." Cynthia tossed her curled head and made a *moue* of annoyance. "Go up and look for yourself." "Better wait for the men," counseled Eleanor Macdermott, and, as if to dismiss the matter, she moved to the door with a shrug. Katy put out a hand to detain her. "Eleanor," she begged, thoroughly perturbed, "hadn't we better do *something*?" Eleanor shrugged again. "Go up and look if you want to," she threw out curtly, evading Katy's hand. "Does it really make so much difference to you?" she added, half in curiosity, half in rebuke. Katy flushed. As a matter of fact, she had been mentally counting the strawberries that could be picked while the group on the porch delayed; her imperious love of pleasure had attached itself to the day's outing, and the invaders in the meadow seemed to her to have been sent by some malign destiny expressly to cross her will. Recovering from her confusion, she saw the Taubs examining her with a certain morose satisfaction, as though to say, Now it has happened and you see where Utopian ideas get you. This complacent scrutiny put her at once on her mettle. The challenge of the pickers would have to be met and answered. And though she longed for her husband or Haines or Macdougal to come and meet it for her, her very isolation, the unfriendliness of her three companions became, as she inwardly debated, a greater incentive to action. Nervous and shy with strangers, fearful of disapproval, unsure of her own motives, she was driven by these qualities to assume an attitude of confidence that would put the others to shame. "I'm going up and speak to them," she announced, just as she had decided that it was wiser not to do so—confronted with any difficult problem, Katy always made two decisions; the second remedying the moral weakness that was disclosed to her by the first. No one tried to deter her, and she set off alone up the hill, hoping to hear behind her the voice of a friendly colonist and assuring herself that the unbroken stillness meant that the pickers were gone.

In all her fears of what was about to happen (the fear of being screamed at, of being abused, of having coarse language used to her, of being impudently flouted), the fear of physical violence did not figure: nor did she imagine that the trespassers would ignore her, for she was accustomed to a great deal of attention. She came into the meadow, therefore, and walked quite decisively to a point almost in the middle. The pickers appeared to be of the very poorest farmer class. "How do you do?" she said, looking at none of them in particular. "We don't mind your picking, but would you leave some of the strawberries for us?" She smiled timidly and went on. "I suppose you've been coming here for years and nobody ever bothered you before, but unfortunately we've bought the place and we're going to be picking ourselves here in about half an hour." The man muttered something and they all stopped picking for a moment, with surly but tentative expressions as though waiting for what she would say next. What they were expecting of course, was for her to pronounce the words, "Get out," or to implement in some manner the declaration of ownership she had just made. And she herself felt that something more was called for, but the pronunciation of those words was simply impossible to her, why, she could not afterwards be sure, whether from the fear of being disobeyed once she had irrevocably given an order, or from some natural democratic feeling which prohibited the brusquerie of such a speech. That anyone would refuse to leave a property on which he was poaching, when the situation was put to him equably, was something so foreign to the stiff pride and self-consciousness of her nature that she could hardly compass what was happening, and stood for a moment rooted to the spot while they watched her, not yet commencing to pick again but making no motion to go. "Won't you leave some for us, please?" she repeated. At this the man snorted, emboldened, it seemed, by her nervousness, and raised his hand abruptly in a rude and half-menacing gesture. To threaten to call the police (the first recourse of the bourgeois mentality) struck her as foolish and futile; imagining that these people read her mind, she dismissed the thought hastily, for she did not wish them to divine how unprotected she was, how unable both morally and physically (would they guess that she had no telephone?) to make an appeal to the law. Mustering all her forces, she turned and walked firmly away from them, as though her mission were completed, and did not quicken her step until just as she gained the road she heard the woman's shrill voice behind her shouting obscene imprecations. Half-dazed and unable to think connectedly, turning her ankles, Katy stumbled homeward, mechanically constructing arguments which she might have used to put the colony's title to the strawberries in terms that would win anyone's sympathy—the rights of legal possession she was ashamed to invoke again. We *need* them, she heard herself pleading. Remembering the hampers of chicken, the young lettuces, and the freezer of ice-cream waiting on the verandah, she felt sure that this exquisite picnic constituted an inalienable right to the delicacy around which it had been planned. Those brutal people up above were incapable of appreciating the strawberries; they would simply cram them down their throats or take them to the market and sell them. This argument, with its aesthetic claim, its appeal, as it were, to the strawberry (By whom would you rather be eaten?) convinced Katy herself; yet the impossibility of using it to *them* as an instrument of gentle persuasion induced in her all at once a feeling of intellectual helplessness, to which force appeared the only answer. "We have got to get them out of there," she exclaimed desperately, running up the porch stairs. "Preston!" she cried, as her husband rose from a lounge chair. *"You* go up and get rid of them!"

Preston's slender back had already stiffened. During Katy's absence, most of the younger colonists had drifted up to the porch, and a quarrel was in progress between them and the older realists as to whether she had done rightly or wrongly in tackling the poachers herself. All the latent hostilities of the past six weeks had sprung into the open, though, as often happens, the disputants had lined up in what would have seemed to be the reverse of their normal positions. The young people, perhaps from loyalty to Preston, were defending Katy's action, while the older members were furiously condemning her for individualistic conduct. No principles were being invoked: Macdermott, Haines, and many of the others had not returned yet; and Francis, the young divine, stood apart with Eleanor Macdermott, following the struggle dispassionately, arms folded, judicious, as though watching a Christmas pantomime or refereeing a game of soccer in the parish yard. Preston, silent and angry, glared steadily at Cynthia Taub; he lost his head quickly in argument, like a young boy in liquor. A zealot of the personal, he did not care who was right. He had always detested the Taubs, and the fact that they were now daring to criticize Katy in his hearing was a piece of effrontery that took his breath away. Katy's suppliant cry went straight to his boyish vanity. Indifferent to the strawberries, not bothering to give or hear reasons, acting principally from defiance, a prime mover with him, he leapt showily over the porch rail and struck off directly up through the fringe of pine forests, disdaining the curved road. The young veteran, who after nearly two months in the colony was still afraid to voice an opinion, now felt encouraged by Preston to do what impulse had been dictating, and without saying

anything to anyone, he hurried to Joe's bed-
room, took his rifle down, slipped out the back
door with it and followed Preston over the hill.
Katy saw him go, but a stupid fatalism held her
silent and she did not express her alarm and
misgiving until he was out of sight.

"Why didn't you stop him?" Taub demanded
roughly, seizing her by the arm and shaking her.
An uncontrollable fear and hatred of violence
gave him a baleful aspect; the watery whites of
his eyes grew bloodshot and he bared his teeth
in a rasp of fury. "I don't know," cried Katy.
"A-a-a-h," cried Taub, dropping her arm, and
mimicking her sarcastically, "*You* don't know,"
and pacing up and down the porch, he repeated
the phrase over and over with varying inflec-
tions of disbelief. Katy bowed her head. Francis
touched her shoulder, absolving. "It seems improbable that he will use it," he said. "Of course
not," said Irene, coming up and taking Katy's
hand soothingly; but no one else spoke. This
young veteran was an unknown quantity to
nearly all of them; he and Irene kept themselves
a little withdrawn from the older people; presumably, they were in love. "Trigger-happy,"

muttered Taub abruptly, having located this term in his portfolio, and as if in answer to his thought there came the sound of a shot and then another and another. Katy screamed and rushed to the edge of the porch; she was certain her husband had been murdered. "You fool," said Taub, grasping at her. "Do you want to be killed too?" Eleanor Macdermott, who had been standing with compressed lips, gestured to Taub to release her. "The children are out there," she acidly reminded him, and Katy, with a new cry of horror, collapsed weeping on the steps. Joe and Mac appeared from the woods with their pails. "What's going on?" Mac demanded. At this moment, Preston and Bill, the veteran, emerged from the direction of the high meadow, talking with great animation and clearly in the most carefree spirits.

"Aw, we just took a pot-shot or two," the veteran called out blithely. "I imagine they'll be going along," remarked Preston in his murmurous voice, coming up to the verandah rail and patting Katy's hand. "Roger," answered Bill. "Mission executed." Both factions on the porch exchanged uncomfortable glances. "But you might have killed someone," exclaimed Harold Sidney plaintively. "Blanks," explained Bill, laughing. "Merely a show of force." "You shot *at* them?" asked Macdermott. "Oh, no," said Preston. "We just passed the time of day and then went off to do some target-practice." Joe's gray face had turned yellowish. Unable to credit his ears, he put a horrified question to Taub, who, arms crossed, sat on the railing, nodding, his lips pursed in Rhadamanthine disapproval. Taub flicked a thumb toward Katy, to indicate the source of the trouble, but Joe ignored the gesture. "You've done a terrible thing," he said solemnly, going up to the two young men and putting a hand on the shoulder of each. "You've driven a man and his family off this property with a gun." "But they were picking our berries; we asked them to leave politely," put in one of the women. "Who did that?" cried Joe, wheeling swiftly around and confronting the others. Katy indicated herself, and Joe dropped backward a step. "I never thought this could happen here," he declared, meting out his words slowly, as if unwillingly, and shaking his hawk head. "Have they gone?" he asked, after a moment of silence. As he turned back to question the young men, his nearsighted eyes for the first time focused on the gun. He had been taking it for granted that it belonged to the veteran, but now, as he came nearer and peered at it, frowning, the unthinkable became a certainty. With a short, violent gesture, he seized it from Bill's shoulder and shoved him to one side roughly as he spun around to the verandah, his jaw tightening. "Who gave him authority to go to my room?" he demanded. There was no answer. "Good," he declared, and without another word turned and marched off to the tool shed, while the colonists waited uneasily. In a few moments, he was back. Striding to the middle of the lawn, where Preston and Bill were still standing, he held something aloft and signaled for attention.

"Here," he announced. "I want you all to see this." He opened his raised hand and disclosed a hinge and a padlock. He passed it slowly before them, pausing for an extra moment to urge it on the veteran's gaze. "Enough said," he declared tersely. "This is going on the door of my room." He took a screwdriver out of his pocket and turned on his heel. There was an awestruck silence. Macdermott scratched his beard and sent a questioning look at the minister. Francis nodded. Mac stepped to the edge of the verandah.

"Wait a minute now, Joe," he called out authoritatively. "That's a side issue. Let's decide now what we're going to do about the pickers." He moved down to the lawn and a group of the others followed him. Margaret, the minister's wife, obeying a quick glance from her husband, went up gaily to Joe and twining her arm in his began to pace the lawn with him; in a few minutes, she had relieved him of the padlock. "Let's get rid of this nasty thing," she cajoled, as if speaking to a child, and before he could resist her, she had tossed it off into the underbrush. "Sure," said Macdermott, joining them, and taking Joe's other arm. "Take it easy," he remonstrated, with a cautionary glance at the verandah, where charge and countercharge were continuing. "Property is theft, you know, ha, ha!" he added, laughing more effusively than he had intended. The business-man's eyes protruded. "Say that again," he demanded.

Macdermott repeated the quotation, more lamely, as he became conscious of a gulf between him and the manufacturer which he had never really noticed before. Joe swung around and looked him searchingly in the eyes. "Do you really believe that?" he asked. Macdermott nodded. Joe turned to the minister's wife. "You too?" he pleaded. "Of course not," said Margaret kindly. "Come now, we must all be good."

With a querulous movement of the shoulders, Macdermott shook off her arm. "Count me out," he advised, his voice sharpening with anger. "We don't stand for the same things, *apparently*." The last word had a sarcastic bitterness which he emphasized by a short, cynical laugh. He was nettled by Margaret's tone and the blandness of her desertion, and was setting out, quite deliberately, to localize the irritation he felt with himself, her, Joe, the intruders up above, Bill and Preston, strawberries, the anomalous, change, by working himself up into a shouting rage, going at it with increasing certainty as his own remarks convinced him that he had something to be angry about. "You pretend to believe in the Gospels!" he burst out, suddenly fierce and vociferous, leveling a forefinger at her as though it contained ammunition. "Francis 'pretends,'" corrected Margaret, with a smile. Macdougal pulled up short in amazement. "Aren't you his wife?" he demanded, losing his sense of grievance in an immediate feeling of intense curiosity—the idea that a husband and wife could hold separate theories of life was as foreign to his comradely practice as the idea of separate bedrooms. "Let's not get personal," said Joe, interrupting him with impatience. "There's a problem up there to be solved." Macdermott, who had not forgotten the intruders, frowningly bit his lips. Remembering that he had entered the scene in the role of mediator, he would, in some way, still have liked to make common cause with the business man, whose hospitable attitude toward the strangers had struck him at first as refreshingly human in comparison with the behavior of his friends. But, as he examined his feelings, somewhat to his surprise he found himself siding more and more with Bill and Preston, and regarding Joe's stern and unrelenting profile with a sharp disfavor. The young men had violated a convention of the commercial world, where the handshake and the banner of welcome were axioms of inter-course—this, Macdermott suddenly divined, was what had shocked the older man and made him now zealous to undo the damage, like the proprietor of a store where a clerk has offended a customer. The idea that the colony's *good will* existed in Joe's mind as a perfectly tangible asset now became shocking in its turn to Macder-mott's bohemianism. He did not justify the young men for resorting to fire-arms, but the fact that the pickers had turned nasty when ad-dressed peaceably by a woman presented, as he further considered it, more and more of a poser.

Faced with the old stickler of what he would do if a foreign soldier were raping Eleanor, he had always taken (jesting) refuge in the story told of an English man of letters—"I should endeavor, sir, to get between them." But to tell the truth, as he ruefully admitted, in interna-tional affairs he felt himself on firmer ground. Had he been present on the verandah, he would probably, like Katy, have gone up and tried to persuade the pickers to content themselves with a modest share. A surly and obdurate refusal was something his mind was not equipped to cope with; morals to him were a chess problem in which the opening gambit elicited a set response, and the errors of modern society he laid simply to failure to use the unconventional opening advocated in his magazine's pages. "Suppose," offered Margaret demurely, "we ask them to join our picnic." Macdermott halted, impressed—the gentle strategies of the vicarage were something new to his experience. "Sure we'll invite them to join us—if we find them there, which I question." And suddenly he began to chuckle. "You've found the non-violent answer," he declared, clapping her fondly on the back. "It's the surest way of getting rid of them."

"We haven't seen the end of this," Taub was prophesying grimly, when the group finally gathered on the porch; his analogical intellect had reverted to the insurrectionary period which he had witnessed as a boy, in his homeland, and he imagined the hotel set on fire, the wells poisoned, the henhouses raided, the bicycle tires punctured by an aroused and vindictive peasantry, set on by the three in the meadow. How quickly he and Cynthia could remove to a place of safety was the principal question in his mind.

"Oh, for Christ's sake, Taub," exclaimed Macdougal. "You're not in feudal Europe." He recalled a statement of Gandhi's that to refuse to fight is best, but that to fight is better than to run—the soldier is superior to the coward; and with the assurance of authority behind him, he advanced into the fray. "Let's show them the power of our numbers," and he picked up a hamper and swung it up on his shoulder.

But the trespassers, as it turned out, had already left the meadow with only the crushed berries in the deep tracks of their tires to show that they had ever been there. It was almost a disappointment to the colonists to find, when they began to pick, no signs of a previous comer; the meadow, with its scattering of late white strawberry flowers, had a look of undisturbed serenity—had the intruders not been seen picking, no one could have believed in their reality; clearly, they had been scared off in time. The excitement of the past half-hour quickly assumed a dreamlike character; the members kept looking back at the car tracks to assure themselves that there had indeed been a danger, and gradually the absence of the strangers began to be felt as a positive embarrassment. Now that the crop was secure, no one felt satisfied with a victory that fell short of an ethical triumph. "Such a fuss over a few little berries," Eva kept exclaiming, as she measured the contents of the baskets. "The big ones are so much nicer— what a pity we couldn't have had them!" For once, she was not corrected. "Now, Mom," said Joe, as she spat a hull disdainfully from her lips, but he was aware suddenly of a comradeship with her which put the others in the cold. Only the children picked with any real enthusiasm. "Those bad people tried to steal our strawberries," a five-year-old was chanting. "Hush," said his mother quickly, looking over her shoulder as though the ghost of the trespassers were lurking off in the pine shadows, ready to take offense. The prize was awarded to Katy in an atmosphere of forced congratulation; she was known to be the best picker, but her proficiency today seemed immoderate.

It was not at first openly acknowledged that the picnic had been spoiled; the morale of the colony was too bruised and shaken by the encounter, but as the lunch hampers were opened and the sharp red wine began to circulate, the members drew apart from each other and, forming small circles, lowered their heads and voices, to allot blame and forgiveness and to moralize on the event. A phase of the colony had ended, everyone privately conceded; something had been lost that was perhaps an essential ingredient—a man can live without self-respect, but a group shatters, dispersed by the ugliness it sees reflected in itself. The distaste felt by some, Susan and Danny Furnas, in particular, was so acute that they questioned the immediate validity of staying on in a colony where such a thing could take place. The fault, in their view, lay with no single person, but with the middle-class composition of the colony, which, feeling itself imperiled, had acted instinctively, as an organism, to extrude the riffraff from its midst. The fact that the incident had occurred spontaneously and almost against the will of the very members who had taken part in it was, to their minds, the most discouraging feature. "It happened too fast for them," Danny's wife put in excusingly. "They didn't have time to think. We should make it a rule that nobody can take it on himself to execute colony business." "Baby, you can never make rules to cover such situations, that's the whole trouble," said Danny. "Nice people like these," he waved a chubby finger, "are always all right, unless you take them off guard. Let's admit, to start with, that these folks have learned a lesson. If, in a couple of weeks, we get some raspberry pickers, you'll see Katy or Cynthia running out with a silver dish—'Would you care to use this?'" he mimicked Cynthia's accent.

Susan and Helen laughed. But a little frown of anxious perplexity wrinkled the fair, thin skin of Susan's forehead. "Still, Danny, that would be an improvement. Don't you think so?" she asked with her usual after-flurry of alarm. Danny's lower lip protruded thoughtfully. "Y-es," he conceded. "I suppose you could say that. But something else will come along, something we can't predict—if we could, you could make a rule for it," he affectionately poked his wife, "and the organism, unprepared, will react to it according to its own rules, the ones it was

169

born with. And then we will have another mass repentance." He yawned and sank back in the grass. "Let's hope that our next visitor will be an escaped convict."

"Let us ask ourselves why we feel bad," said Leo equably to Macdermott. "True, we behaved unsociably; that can't be denied. But aren't we being a little pharisaical in taking all the blame to ourselves? Supposing these pickers had been nice, co-operative people, and when Katy went up to talk to them, they had picked a few berries and left—how would we feel? We would feel fine, eh?" Macdermott uncertainly nodded. "Now suppose we had let them bully us into giving up the berries, how would we feel?" "Bad," admitted Macdermott. "So therefore we feel bad because the pickers are bad people, is that right?" "Yes," said Macdermott. "What follows?" "Why, nothing," said Leo. "Let's just get it clear what we are depressed about." Macdermott fitted a cigarette into his holder and sat thoughtfully looking out toward the black range of the Taconics, following with his mind's eye the Appalachian system down the rocky spinal column of Eastern North America, touching the anthracite ribs of Pennsylvania, the bituminous back of West Virginia, the dim extremities of the Great Smokies, and his heart, as he smoked, grew large with a pure and impersonal regret.

Katy and Preston Norell sat with Bill and Irene, conversing sparsely and coldly, and getting disagreeably drunk as the jug passed between them. They felt that the colony was on the verge of dissolution unless some tremendous effort were made at once to save it, but their imaginations were unequal to formulating what this should be. Irene looked to her teacher for a sign that she might follow, and, failing to receive one, slumped into a childish melancholy. She set her thin lips and ceased to speak altogether, blaming Katy, the colony, and everyone older than herself for their inadequacy to her personal standards; all the sympathy for the disaster she was envisioning, she lavished youthfully on herself. The faint wrinkles by Katy's eyes, the few threads of grey in her brown hair, presented themselves in this northern noonday with an ugly distinctness. Irene studied them without pity, as if they were a moral blemish

171

her teacher had been concealing from her and which she now took a mordant satisfaction in unmasking. "We're going for a walk," she suddenly announced, pulling herself to her feet, and brushing her skirt fastidiously. She took Bill's arm and they strode off on their long legs into the forest, leaving their dessert uneaten.

Taub, perceiving that the Norells were alone, made his way slowly over to them. Restored to kindliness by the lunch he had eaten and by the assurances of the majority that there was nothing more to fear from the poachers, he felt a desire to make amends for his hastiness on the verandah and also to point the moral so aptly illustrated by the incident. No sense of reproach remained in him. "Human nature, Katy," he remonstrated playfully, wagging a finger at her. "That's the thing you leave out." "Mine, you mean, or those pickers?" asked Katy, sitting up. "Both!" enunciated Taub, with the air of a master theorist. "Force," he declared softly. "That's what we all understand. You have it in *you*, Katy," he continued, almost in a whisper, and with a hypnotic stare of his black eyes. "You gave yourself away on the porch."

Taub, too, was a little drunk and was swaying slightly on his feet, as he leaned caressingly down toward her, his eyes damp and glittering, like a magnetic confessor of women. Katy felt slightly repelled. "You had to use force to get rid of them—admit it for once, Katy." He leaned still closer to her, urgent, masterful, persuasive.

"You conceive the problem incorrectly," she declared, straightening herself up and articulating with that unnatural distinctness that betrays that the speaker has been drinking. Her mind, however, was lucid. "If the problem is to get rid of the berry pickers, it follows that force is the answer—to that extent, you are right. Ultimately, it will have to be resorted to, if they will not respond to moral coercion, which is simply force still withheld. But," she went on, growing more excited, "supposing there is no problem, but simply an event: the berry-pickers are in the meadow; the sun is in the sky. If you do not wish to eject them, there is no problem, there is only an occurrence."

Taub shrugged; he did not understand what she was getting at. "Do you know why the saints and the moral philosophers call for a rule of abstinence and chastity?" she asked eagerly, as if this question had been a perpetual source of difficulty to her listener. Taub shrugged again. "I've never been sympathetic to it either," admitted Katy, "but just now I've seen what they mean. The body is not evil, and the body's objects are not evil—the strawberries are ethically neutral. But if these corporeal things become the object of a mental desire, the result is an impurity, which is evil. A mental desire of material things is always bad—sex becomes pornography; hunger becomes greed or gourmandism—you follow me?" Taub nodded succinctly. "The mind, properly speaking, must desire only its own objects, love, formal beauty, virtue. But if the mind is not trained to distinguish its objects from the body's, it confuses the two. It constructs the whim for the strawberries into an ethical demand; it appears, then, to the mind that it *needs* the strawberries and is therefore morally justified in any action it may take to secure them. But since the strawberries are a material thing, they can, in the last analysis, only be secured by force, which is physical necessity. If we had been hungry," she added, "there would have been nothing inconsonant in putting up a fight for the strawberries. However, since our desire for them was mental, one strawberry would have served as well as a hundred, and there should have been no need of disputing possession, for two minds can hold an object simultaneously."

Taub ruminated for a moment. The strawberries of Carpathia-Ruthenia stirred restlessly in his imagination, as though to say, Yes, we are here. "There is something in what you say," he remarked cautiously. "Asceticism," continued Katy, "is simply an extreme method of accomplishing this necessary separation—you browbeat and degrade one half. To train the mind is more difficult," she interjected with a flash of sadness. "The problem for the colony is not to confuse its material triumphs with the triumph of its idea. There is nothing here," she gestured vaguely into the blue distance, "which the colony cannot do without. That is what we should be concerned to demonstrate. We've shown that we can do without cars and electricity, but we ought also to show that we can do without our butter churns and oil lamps and go back to washing-machines and Mixmasters, if it seems necessary. The colony must not be identified with its implements." Taub frowned at the last word, which recalled him to the sphere of his ascendancy. "Historically," he stated, "man is shaped by his economy and his environment." "Then let us get out of history," retorted Katy rather sharply. Will's face abruptly hardened. "Try it," he suggested with a fleering laugh. "Know yourself, Katy," he advised her, bringing a large hand down on her shoulder. "You forget that one little thing, the first rule of your philosophers." He teetered heavily toward her, and Preston, who had been half-listening, looked up in sudden surprise. He was not especially interested in her conversation with Taub, for he knew that Katy was sad and that whenever she was sad she had many new ideas and tried to reform herself and him also. He considered her, on the whole, to be well enough as she was, being himself a little weary of this quest for perfection, which only meant upsetting their habits for a short time and buying, usually, several new objects which would gradually fall into disrepair. This time, he had begun to suppose, she would be asking to send for a prayer-rug. Glancing up at her, however, he felt a quick rush of uxorious pride and reassurance, for her face was lively and sensible, and as he watched her, she commenced to smile broadly. "I?" she said to Taub. "I'm the worst of all. Who did you suppose I was talking about?" Taub gave a short grunt, but, not wishing to appear disconcerted, he decided to treat this as an admission wrung from her by his thumb-screw of analysis. He hastily became genial. "Don't flatter yourself, Katy," he said kindly. "You're *just like everybody else*." And imparting to these final words the sonority of a black benediction, he left her, before she should use the occasion to interpose any more of her thoughts.

Katy lay back on the meadow grass and enlaced her fingers with Preston's. For some curious reason, she felt suddenly happy and contented. Her conscience no longer troubled her, for in this luminous interlude between drunkenness and sobriety she had divined that her hunger for goodness was an appetency not of this world and not to be satisfied by actions, which would forever cheat its insistencies. She recognized, with a new equanimity, that her behavior would never suit her requirements, not to mention the requirements of others; and while she did not propose to sink, therefore, into iniquity or to institutionalize her frailties in the manner of the realist faction, still, seen in this unaccustomed light, the desire to *embody* virtue appeared a shallow and vulgar craving, the refracted error of a naïve and acquisitive culture which imagined that there was nothing —beauty, honor, titles of nobility, charm, youth, happiness—which persistency could not secure. And the colony itself, as she considered it, with its energy, its uncertainty, its euphoria, its cycles of recession and recovery, seemed also to have been prismatically imaging the galvanic world down below—in the social field, it had been treating itself as a kind of factory or business for the manufacture and export of morality. The spirits of the colonists rose and fell with the market-quotation of the enterprise; at the moment, its stock was very low. These crises, she foresaw, would shake the colony to pieces, unless a new pattern were discovered.

178

Ultimately, Utopia would fail; that was to be expected. But it might survive for many months or for years, if the production of a commodity more tangible than morality could be undertaken. Morality did not keep well; it required stable conditions; it was costly; it was subject to variations, and the market for it was uncertain. Cheese, wine, books, glass, furniture—idly Katy's mind considered the possibilities a factory might offer, certain that somewhere in this practical realm lay the colony's true security. But she said nothing aloud, for it seemed to her presumptuous to come forward with a panacea. This was not her part. Moreover, it was still too early. Much remained yet to be suffered, many failures, many humiliations. The colony must settle like a house onto its foundations, creaking and groaning and sighing. Certain visitors must leave it. In the warm sun her eyelids began to droop. Leo's plan, she remembered; the pamphlet—half-starting up in fright and then sinking back, as she recalled that they had not yet betrayed it; not a day had elapsed since its proposal. The sun beat down on her eyelids, making a red darkness, and suddenly, on the screen

of her vision, a scene from the future was pro-
jected. She saw Jim Haines——whom she had
been missing, as she suddenly realized, during
the last hour of the picnic——dressed in his city
tweed suit, walking in a pair of orange-brown
shoes with a peculiar sidelong gait toward the
shed; the light was grey—it was early in the
morning. "Hello, there, Katy," his voice mum-
bled as if directly into her ear. "Glad I came
across you. Meant to mention it earlier. Martha
and I are leaving." And then immediately the
rear of the Haines' nondescript black car was
disappearing bumpily up the driveway, the
trunk partly open and a kiddie-coop tied with
rope and a lumpy bag of laundry protruding.
As Katy stood watching, endeavoring to call,
"Stop," the struggle for articulation brought
her back to consciousness. She knew at once
that she had been warned of a clear and present
danger. Jim Haines was about to abandon them,
like a sorely beset husband; the doubt, the hesi-
tation, the scruple had worn out his stock of
magnanimity. And yet if he went, all went; the
man willing to be shown departed, having seen
enough. She made a movement to rise to go to

find him; appeasement, explanations, cajolery could hold him a little longer. Her husband's fingers, squeezing her own gently, deterred her, as if sentient of her thoughts. Haines could not he held; equivocal, slippery, indeterminate, the citizen of open opinions evaded the theoretician's grasp and returned stealthily to his habits, as if to a gentleman's club. On the wide canvas of the meadow, crowded with bright, grotesque types, the apostles of a Breughelesque vision, eating, drinking, disputing, elongated or vastly swollen, she saw the average man stealing out of one corner of the picture, a guilty finger to his lips. And rising apologetically from nearer the center, Joe, an itinerant harvester, was sharpening his scythe, tarrying briefly before the journey to new fields of conquest. Who would remain at the banquet? Drowsily, she began to count on her fingers: Macdermott, Susan, Francis; Preston, Danny, Leo. Taub? she asked herself; then confusing her fingers with her husband's she lost track of the number and assentingly fell asleep.